# The MAGNIFICENT Mya Tibbs

## MYA IN THE MIDDLE

# Also by Crystal Allen

# The MAGNIFICENT Mya Tibbs

## MYA IN THE MIDDLE

## CRYSTAL ALLEN

Illustrations by Eda Kaban

BALZER + BRAY

*An Imprint of* HarperCollins*Publishers*

Balzer + Bray is an imprint of HarperCollins Publishers.

The Magnificent Mya Tibbs: Mya in the Middle
Text copyright © 2018 by Crystal Allen
Illustrations copyright © 2018 by Eda Kaban
For information address HarperCollins Children's Books,
a division of HarperCollins Publishers,
195 Broadway, New York, NY 10007.
www.harpercollinschildrens.com

ISBN 978-0-06-283939-8

Typography by Carla Weise
18 19 20 21 22   CG/LSCH   10 9 8 7 6 5 4 3 2 1
❖
First Edition

To Andrew, Clara, Michael, and Paula.
I love you.

# The MAGNIFICENT Mya Tibbs

## MYA IN THE MIDDLE

# Chapter One

There is a huge giggle sitting in the back of my throat, trying to get out, but it needs to stay there for a few more seconds. I swing my legs under the table as Mom grabs the comb and brush. She kisses my forehead and asks the same question she asks me every morning.

"How many braids would you like today, Mya?"

I know she's expecting me to say two or three, but I fool her.

"Twenty-one."

My giggle escapes when I hear her mumbling, "Why on earth would Mya want twenty-one braids?"

I give her a hint. "Come on, Mom. Think! It happens the same time every year, in the same month, and I always ask for the same number of braids."

I can almost hear the smile spread across her face. "Is it March twenty-first already?"

She gets two thumbs up. "Ding, ding, ding!"

I hand her my box of red, yellow, blue, white, and purple hair decorations so she can add one to the end of each braid. When she's finished, my hair will remind everybody of the first day of spring! Mom parts my hair in three sections.

"Okay, I can make twenty-one braids, but a good taradiddle might help me work faster."

I answer in my best country-and-western voice. "Comin' right up, little lady! Way back, a hundred years ago, in December, the good citizens of Bluebonnet sat on their porches in shorts and T-shirts, drinking sweet tea and eating barbecue as the sun shone down on her favorite town. Suddenly a dust storm whirled across Spring Street, and the gallop of a horse got everybody's attention. *Clickety-dump, clickety-dump, clickety-dump.* A villain appeared with icicles in his eyebrows and beard, riding a horse with snow in its mane. He wore a huge white coat, full of cold air. He unzipped his coat and released a brutal freeze on Bluebonnet.

"'Run for your life! It's Old Man Winter!' someone shouted."

Mom is already finished braiding my hair in the back. She moves to my left side and fakes a shiver. "Now I'm cold. But go ahead, Mya. I want to know what's going to happen."

I continue. "The sun tried to fight by zapping that villain with her rays, but Old Man Winter was too much for her. Sun ran away, leaving Bluebonnet in a cold tizzy.

"Two months later, the sun came back! She beamed fiery darts at Old Man Winter and his horse, melting their icicles until they both got out of town! Somebody wrote about it in the newspaper and called the twenty-first day of March the first day of spring, and dedicated it to the sun coming back. Sometimes it's celebrated on the twentieth, too."

Mom hugs my shoulders. "That was a really good taradiddle, young lady. Once I plait your hair on the right, you'll have a headful of springtime."

Dad and Nugget sit at the breakfast table reading the *Bluebonnet Tribune* and eating breakfast. Even though my brother's real name is Micah, everybody calls him Nugget because his skin is brown and his head is shaped like a chunk of chicken. He thinks he's named after a piece of gold. Suddenly Dad's voice gets loud.

"This is ridiculous!" He turns to Mom. "Monica, did you see that the price of corn is up? I'm already paying top dollar for it. How am I supposed to make my special horse and cattle mix with corn prices through the roof?"

Mom continues to braid my hair. "I'm sure you'll figure something out."

"It's all about supply and demand, Dad," I say.

Nugget joins the conversation. "I'm sure the price increase is due to the flood last year."

"I bet the flooding caused a bad crop of corn. So the corn producer raised the price because he lost a lot of money when the corn didn't grow," I say.

Nugget nods. "And in this agricultural region, corn is a huge commodity." He puts down the newspaper and grins at me. "You must be studying economics in Mrs. Davis's class."

"Yeah. It's really interesting," I say, grinning back.

"I know. I studied it last year," he says.

Mom finishes my braids. I touch them, and they feel straight and perfect. I give Mom a big hug before *ka-clunk*ing over to the table.

Dad puts both hands in the air. "Wait a minute,

time out, stop for a second."

His eyes ping-pong back and forth from me to my brother. "When did you two learn about economics? Mya, you're in fourth grade, right?"

I roll my eyes. "Come on, Dad. Don't you remember a couple of weeks ago when I gave you that note from Mrs. Davis about me needing twenty-five dollars for our economics lessons? You gave it to me, remember? Anyway, let me explain something to you about economics." I take his hand and try to be as gentle as possible with what I'm about to say. "Try to stick with me on this, Dad. See, the supply of corn is low, but the demand for it is still high. You're stuck in the middle because you buy corn from the growers and supply it to your customers. I know it's tough being a middleman."

He shrugs at Mom. "When did they start teaching economics in elementary school?"

"I don't know," says Mom, shrugging back.

Dad's voice is still loud as he talks to my brother. "Let's just move on. There's nothing I can do about it. Nugget, I need that inventory list today."

My brother nods. "I'll have it done by the time you get home from work."

I don't know what an inventory list is, but I can't believe how angry Dad is over the price of corn. If he doesn't stop yelling, he's going to wake up. . . .

*"Waaah! Waaaaaah!"*

Too late. Macey's awake.

"I'll get her, Darrell," says Mom.

Dad pushes back from the table. "No, I woke her up, I'll go get her," he says, walking toward the playpen near the kitchen.

I shake my head from left to right and feel my braids swing and my hair clips clack together. It sounds perfect! I'm on my way to find a mirror when I hear . . .

"Look at my baby girl!"

That's what Dad's called me since I was Macey's age. I pose for him with a big smile on my face. But my smile slowly fades when I realize the worst thing ever.

He wasn't talking to me.

My braids stop swinging. Inside my belly, I can feel my guts bubbling as I watch Dad hold Macey so close that their noses touch. She coos at him. He chuckles. Mom giggles, too.

"I sure wish I knew what she was saying when she coos like that," says Dad.

I know what she's saying. I've spent a lot of time studying baby sounds, leg kicks, and face expressions, so I can figure out what she wants. It's like I graduated from Goo-Goo University or the College of Coo. I understand Macey better than anyone else in the family.

If she pouts before she cries and makes an "I stink" face, that means she needs her diaper changed. If she cries and kicks her legs like she's swimming, I know she wants me to pick her up. And when she cries and then sticks her fist in her mouth, I know she's ready to eat. Even though my little sister has only been here for six months, I already love her, and she loves me. We're perfect sisters.

"She wants her diaper changed," I say.

Mom nods. "I'm sure you're right. She hasn't been changed since early this morning."

Dad shuffles into the nursery, holding Macey. Mom's right behind him. Neither one of them says goodbye, or have a good day. And worse, they forget to give me a hug. I don't remember them ever not hugging me, or not wishing me a good day before. Does this mean I'm going to automatically have a bad day? I look at my brother. He picks up his spoon.

"Hey, Mya, watch this."

Nugget opens his mouth, blows air on his spoon— and then he sticks the spoon to his nose! And it stays without him holding it! I can't help but laugh.

"You are so silly," I say.

"I'm being nosy," he says.

I laugh again. I can always count on Nugget to make me feel better.

He nods toward the door. "Go do a weather test."

"Have you done one yet?" I ask.

"Yes, and you're going to be really happy."

Since December it's been freezing cold in the mornings, and I've had to run back inside to get my heavy brown coat, gloves, and hat. But today the weather feels like love. It's as if the sun knows my name. *Come let me shine on you today, baby girl!*

Yee-haw! I've got a happy rhythm running from my braids to my boots as I walk back into the house, grinning. "It feels awesome out there!"

"I know! And it's going to get warmer. I'm only going to wear a hoodie," says Nugget.

"Wear the black one. It makes you look cool. I'm getting my jean jacket," I say.

I chug the last of my orange juice, grab my jacket and my backpack, and hit the sidewalk. I forget about Dad and Macey. All I can think of is what I'm seeing and feeling outside.

## Chapter Two

Soon we're at the front doors of the best school on the planet—Young Elementary. Mr. Winky, our principal, greets us.

"Well, good morning, good morning. It's a beautiful day outside. Spring has sprung, but hurry to class before the bell has rung! We must be on time. Yes, yes, yes we must!"

Mr. Winky likes to say yes a lot because it's our school's initials—Y.E.S. Usually it's cool to hear him do his yes, yes, yes, but some days, I wish he'd stop after "Good morning."

Nugget hurries down the fifth-grade hall, and

I *ka-clunk* down the fourth. As soon as I enter my classroom, Mrs. Davis greets me.

"Good morning, Mya."

I pretend I've got on a cowgirl hat and tip the front of it at her. "Mornin', ma'am."

She smiles. "Mornin', Miss Mya! What do you think about this weather?"

"I love it. Can we have two recesses today instead of one?"

"I'm sure that won't happen, but I like how you think," she says, still smiling.

I nod and keep *ka-clunk*ing, because the coolest thing about being in fourth grade is the Cave. Mrs. Davis said that years ago, the Cave was actually an extra classroom, but a few years in a row, it wasn't needed. They gave the extra space to the fourth graders! The other classrooms just have hooks in the back of the room to hang up stuff.

Inside the Cave, each of us has our very own cabinet where we put our backpacks, lunches, and supplies. In front of the cabinets are benches to sit on to tie shoes, take off rain boots, or even just sit and relax! There are speakers wired into the walls. Mrs. Davis lets us listen to DJ Cool Breezy on the radio in the morning before the bell rings. He plays all kinds of good music, and when a popular song comes on, we all dance and sing along.

There's a lot going on in the Cave when I get there. The twins, Starr and Skye, are playing hand-clapping games with Naomi. Kenyan, David, Lisa, and Johnny talk sports. Everybody's having a good time. I head to my cabinet to put my backpack and jacket inside.

DJ Cool Breezy is playing some good music, and I can't help but move my feet. I hear my hair clips clacking as I get my groove on. The twins are the first to greet me.

"Hey, Mya," says Skye.

"Hi, Mya," says Starr.

"I like your braids," says Skye.

"Your braids are hot," says Starr.

"Thanks. Who won the clapping game?"

"Naomi," says Skye.

"Naomi won," says Starr.

"I remember that time when your mom braided our hair," says Skye.

"We were hanging out at your house on a Saturday, and your mom braided our hair. It was awesome," says Starr.

"We looked fab," says Skye.

"Totally fab," says Starr.

Naomi joins us. She's standing next to Starr

because they don't like people standing between them. That's how close they are.

"Naomi, Mya's braids are banging, don't you think?" asks Skye.

"Don't you think they bang?" asks Starr.

My eyes slowly roll toward Naomi, my number-one biggest enemy on the planet. We haven't been friends since Spirit Week, seven months ago. I know she's going to say something horrible about my braids. I'm already thinking of something smart-aleck to say back to her when Naomi shrugs and my words get stuck between my brain and my mouth.

"Yeah, they look okay, I guess," she says.

What? I was all ready for Naomi to call me Snake Braids or Mop Head, but she didn't.

"Can I move your hair decorations around?" asks Skye.

"I know exactly what you're going to do, Skye," says Starr. "I'll help."

The twins unclip my hair decorations and move them to different braids. After a minute or two, they stop, take a step back, and stare at my hair.

"I think we nailed it, don't you?" asks Skye.

"Definitely nailed it. Don't you think we nailed it, Naomi?" asks Starr.

"I already told you what I think. I'm going into the classroom," she says.

That's what I expected her to say. Now she sounds like the Naomi I know. I shake my head from side to side to make my braids swing in the air. "I don't know what you two did, but I'm sure I'll love it."

"Hey, we stole an idea from you," says Skye.

"But we're not real thieves," says Starr.

"You know how you like to use your braids to count down days?" asks Skye.

"You know what we're talking about, right?" asks Starr.

I shrug. "Yeah, what about it?"

"We decided to paint our nails to count down the days until our birthday!" says Skye.

"We're painting our fingernails and toenails one at a time until the big day," says Starr.

I look at their toes and notice their big toes have red nail polish on them, but all the other nails are bare. I ball up my fist and give both of them bumps. "That's awesome!"

"Thanks for not thinking we're thieves," says Skye.

"Thanks, Mya," says Starr.

Naomi comes back. "I almost forgot to tell you

something. I heard my mom talking to your mom last night. I think your mom is going to hire my mom as a party planner! That makes sense, especially since our families are practically best friends."

My braids feel tighter than they did a few seconds ago. I know a lie when I hear one. There's no way Skye and Starr's parents are better friends with Naomi's parents than with mine.

The twins' dad owns a camera and UFO-sighting shop right next door to Tibbs's Farm and Ranch Store. Our dads have lunch together at the Burger Bar. Our moms go to church together, and they belong to the same book club.

"Yay! We want a party! We're going to be double digits," says Skye.

"Double numbers just like we're double people," says Starr.

My best friend, Connie Tate, comes over. Naomi leaves, but not before a very awkward staredown between them. Connie's been enemies with Naomi even longer than I have.

Connie gives the twins and me hugs. "It feels amazing outside, doesn't it?"

"We took our time this morning. It's so warm out," says Skye.

"Slow-walked all the way to school," says Starr.

"Nugget and I did the same thing," I say.

Connie nods. "I wish we could start the morning with recess. I would totally skip out on painting and go outside."

Connie is the best painter in Bluebonnet. Even though she's only in the fourth grade, she's won contests, and she does all the posters for Mr. Winky for things like Spirit Week, Open House, and holidays.

The warning bell rings, and we all rush out of the Cave and into our seats. After the Pledge of Allegiance and the moment of silence, everything seems normal until Mrs. Davis stands in front of her desk with a box in her hand. It's not decorated. It doesn't look fancy. It's a box, like a shoebox.

"Class, on April ninth, our town, Bluebonnet, turns one hundred years old! And to celebrate spring's arrival, and Bluebonnet's birthday, we're going to add those two things to our focus on economics."

"We were born on April Fool's Day! We'll be ten years old!" says Skye.

"Perfect numbers!" says Starr.

"You were born on April first? That's kinda cool!" yells Johnny.

David raises his hand. "There's a huge party going down at the park next month to celebrate

Bluebonnet turning a hundred. I heard my parents talking about it."

Mrs. Davis nods. "That's true. And we're all invited!"

There's clapping, lots of *whoop-whoops*, and fist bumps. I'm thinking it sounds like the party has already started! Mrs. Davis holds up two fingers. That's her signal to calm down, and we do. She paces very slowly in front of her desk as she talks.

"We've come to the end of our study of business and economics. It's time to put what we've learned into action. So, boys and girls, today we're going to start our new project. It's called Spring into a New Business for Bluebonnet! Each student—or you can pair up with a friend—will create a new company, in an effort to bring more business to Bluebonnet. You must keep your business thriving until the day before the big birthday celebration for our town's one hundredth birthday, and you must use the twenty-five dollars you brought from home to buy your supplies."

Mrs. Davis holds up a bunch of envelopes. "Each of you has an envelope with twenty-five dollars enclosed, and I have all of those envelopes right here in my hand. You pick the business you want to start. Choose anything!"

David's looking around the room as if something's wrong. "What? Are you serious, Mrs. Davis? We can start our own businesses?"

"Anything I want?" asks Kenyan.

"Anything!" she says. "And, I've decided to add a little extra money to your envelopes. I'm going to give each of you ten thousand dollars."

Kenyan falls out of his chair. Lisa's trying to talk, but she keeps sneezing. Johnny raises his hand and talks before Mrs. Davis calls on him.

"Did you say you're going to give each of us ten thousand dollars?"

She grins. "Yep. That's what I said. I've got all the money in this box."

I can't hold it in. "Holy moly! This is boo-yang! I'm going to buy me a horse!"

"I'm buying an art studio," says Connie.

"I'm getting a car," says David.

"I'm going to buy a hot-dog stand!" says Michael.

Mrs. Davis grins. "Okay, let's settle down. You're acting like you've never had ten thousand dollars before."

We're all laughing. My legs swing under my desk, and mine aren't the only ones as we wait for Mrs. Davis to make us rich! She walks over to the first row and hands a thick envelope to David. Then she hands another thick envelope to Lisa. David's shaking his head. Lisa, too. They must be in shock. By the time she gets to me, I'm ready to take off like a rocket! I open my envelope and look inside.

Good gravy in the navy.

It's Monopoly money.

# Chapter Three

*P*OP! *Clickety-dump, clickety-dump.*

That's the sound of the horse I was going to buy galloping right out of my thoughts. I've got an envelope full of gold, beige, green, blue, yellow, pink, and white money. That won't even buy me a fake horse. I look over my shoulder at Connie. She's staring at her money like she's in shock. For a quick second I almost burst out laughing. But right now, I think I'm the only person on the planet who's finding humor in this rotten situation. Mrs. Davis puts the top back on her box and stands in front of us.

"Each of you has ten thousand dollars in play

money, and twenty-five dollars in real cash. You're going to have to start a business with it. Tomorrow we will talk about how to use your real cash, and what to do with your Monopoly money."

A few minutes ago, we were so excited that we almost lost our minds. Now we're slumping in our chairs, thinking, How in the world are we going to open a business with ten thousand dollars? We have to pay employees, buy supplies, pay rent for an office or a store to sell our products. All that stuff costs money. We have to pay for electricity for lights, and maybe water if we have a bathroom in our store, or a sink, or a water fountain.

After what Mrs. Davis has taught us about economics, we all know that ten thousand dollars is like only having ten dollars.

"I'll be the banker and collect all monies for start-up costs," says Mrs. Davis. "Most of you will need a loan, and I'm willing to give you one if you can show me your business plan and why you would need more money."

Mary Frances raises her hand. "I don't even know what kind of business I want to start."

"That's okay," says Mrs. Davis. "You don't need to know that right now. And class, I will allow you to have a business partner, only one, and that partner must be one of your classmates. This would be a great opportunity to combine your resources. However, I want to see evidence of both partners working to make the business successful. Begin thinking about what you'll need to start a business and what it will take to keep your business going. Before we go to lunch, I want each of you to put your money in your cabinet. Relax, class—this is going to be fun!"

It's dead-people quiet in the room.

The rest of the morning drags by. I'm in a hurry to get outside because I don't want the sun to go away before I get a chance to have some fun with my friends! We've all been waiting a long time for this day, and it's finally here! When the first lunch bell rings, we line up as quickly as we can. Mrs. Davis smiles as she watches us do our best to behave.

There's no talking at lunch because conversation slows down our eating. Connie and I usually sit at a table by ourselves, but today we're sitting with Skye and Starr. We don't get to go outside until everybody is finished. When the bell rings to end lunch, there's not one tray on the table. We all line up near the doors. The sun is beaming outside. This is going to be awesome!

As soon as the doors open, we dash out to the

playground. Connie's usually painting in her special room during recess, but not today. Lots of my classmates scream with happiness. Some run and can't seem to stop! Nugget and his friends shoot baskets, while jump ropes turn and hand-clapping games begin with a song. "Cinder-ella dressed in yel-la . . ."

Connie takes my hand and leads me to our favorite tree. Her face has a lot of worry on it as she barely talks above a whisper. "Mya, I need to tell you something. The other day the mayor's secretary called our house and asked me to draw and paint a picture for the big Bluebonnet party at the park. It's supposed to be a picture that shows why Bluebonnet is so special."

"Jambalaya, Connie! That's awesome. What are you going to draw?"

"I don't know. I'm not feeling it yet. Hopefully something will come to me soon. You wanna jump rope? Play hopscotch? Play a clapping game? We only have fifteen more minutes."

I shrug. "Whatever. I'm just happy to be outside without a heavy coat on. Can you believe Mrs. Davis gave us an envelope full of fake money?"

"I was upset when I opened it."

I can't keep the giggle in my mouth. Connie joins

me, and now we're not upset about the fake money anymore.

"Let's play a clapping game," I say.

Soon Connie and I have a long clapping game going, because neither of us is messing up. We've never gone this long before! Mrs. Davis blows the whistle. We stop, and we hug each other in victory.

"Should have timed it," says Connie.

"I know. That could have been a world record."

"I think it was your braids. They look really awesome. And to think, one day your mom is going to have to do the same thing for Macey, too."

I nod and smile, but the memory of this morning comes back in a hurry. I love my baby sister, but when Dad called her baby girl, it hurt. Maybe it wasn't a big deal to him.

But it was to me.

Maybe it was an accident. It's possible that Dad just made a mistake! Yes, that's it! He was so mad about those corn prices that he accidentally called Macey baby girl.

As I walk back to class, I put a different kind of plan together. I'm going to wear a big grin and be as happy as I can be, in case the price of corn hasn't gone down before I get home. And when Dad gets home from work, I'll tell him everything about my day and won't leave out one thing. He loves that, and sometimes he even puts me on his knee as I talk. But he always calls me baby girl when I talk to him about my day at school.

Back in class, Mrs. Davis ties math into our business plans. In history, we talk about some of the first businesses in Texas. By the time the bell rings, I'm totally ready to get out of that classroom.

Nugget talks all the way home, but I'm not listening. Finally he swipes my braids to get my attention. They swing on my head before coming to a stop.

"What'd you do that for?" I ask.

"I've been talking to you since we left school, and you haven't said a word. Did you get in trouble or something?"

"No. I've got something important on my mind, and I don't want to forget."

Nugget opens the front door, and I grin so hard that my cheeks hurt, because that is what I want Mom to see as soon as we walk into the house.

Nugget yells from the door. "Mom? We're home!"

There's a pile of laundry on the couch. Macey's toys cover the floor. Normally, I would smell something cooking for dinner, but all I smell is baby stuff like diapers and lotion.

Mom rushes into the living room with her finger

pressed to her lips. "Macey's asleep! Please be quiet, okay?"

I cut my eyes to Nugget. He's staring at Mom, too, because she's still in her pajamas. I whisper to her, "Are you feeling okay? Do you need some help?"

She shakes her head. "No, no, I've been really busy with Macey today. She got two shots at the pediatrician's during her six-month checkup. That made her grumpy and she threw up on my blouse. So I put my pajamas back on as soon as I got home. I haven't had an opportunity to do much of anything but take care of her. She finally fell asleep in her playpen. Please take off your shoes and be extra quiet, okay?"

This isn't supposed to be quiet time. This is supposed to be "So Mya, tell me all about your day" time. By the look on my brother's face, he doesn't like this "be quiet" stuff either.

I pull off my boots, Nugget takes off his Nikes, and we tiptoe in our socks. I follow Mom into the kitchen and whisper to her as she places four chicken breasts in the oven.

"Today we finally got to go outside without heavy winter coats, and—"

Mom waves at me. "Not now, Mya. I need to get

dinner finished before your dad gets home. And I need to get out of these pajamas. Tell me during family time after dinner."

Firecrackers. I want to tell Mom now, but I'll wait. "Okay," I say.

I check on Macey on the way out of the kitchen. She's beautiful, and I love her so much. I wish she was awake, because I want to talk to her. I look back at Mom. She's stopped what she was doing and stares at Macey with a smile, then signals me to come back to her in the kitchen. I'm thinking she's going to hug me or something, but instead she whispers in my ear.

"Tell your brother to work on finishing the inventory list for the store, because your dad is going to want it as soon as he gets home."

My eyebrows get closer to each other as my head tilts to the side, and I whisper back. "When did Nugget start doing the inventory list? He's not even an inventor! Actually, I'm probably better at inventing stuff than he is."

Mom giggles. When she sees that I'm not laughing, she stops and explains.

"Nugget's not inventing anything. Supplies are called inventory. Your brother's been keeping up with that for your dad and me since January. He also separates the store receipts to get us ready for tax season. Nugget has a special talent for business."

Now that she mentions it, I remember inventory being one of my economics spelling words, but it was so long ago that I forgot. I nod to let Mom know I heard her, but I still wait a few seconds, to make sure I don't miss a hug. But she doesn't look my way as she talks.

"Mya, go tell Nugget what I told you. Do you have homework?"

"Yes, ma'am," I say, and leave the kitchen.

All this time I was working on a plan to make sure Dad remembered that I'm his baby girl. I should have been working on a plan for Mom, too. She doesn't even have time to hear about my day. All she cares about is making sure I tell Nugget to do the inventory list.

Dad owns Tibbs's Farm and Ranch Store on Main Street. His great-great-grandfather bought land in Bluebonnet and started the family business. And then it kept getting handed down like an old pair of boots. Now the store belongs to Dad.

I grab the cordless phone from the living room, head upstairs, knock on Nugget's door, and give him Mom's message. He nods, but as he tries to shut his door, I put my hand on it.

"Why didn't you tell me you were doing inventory for Mom and Dad?"

He seems annoyed. "What's the big deal? You want to do it?"

"No, I was curious why no one told me about it."

His face changes from annoyed to angry. "So now you have to know everything?"

Nugget doesn't give me time to answer before closing his door. I walk to my room and close my door, too. I pace the floor. My brother thinks he's special just because he's working for Mom and Dad! Who does he think he is, talking to me like that! Yes! I do think I should know everything that's going on in this house. It's my house, too! I don't know what his problem is, but if I find out that Mom, Dad, and Nugget are keeping secrets from me, I'm going to throw a fit, and it's not going to be pretty.

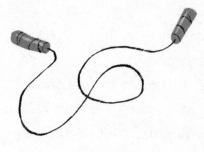

# Chapter Four

Instead of studying or doing homework, I decide to practice my lassoing, to help me calm down. I open my bottom drawer and take out five stuffed animals: a longhorn cow, two horses, one goat, and a sheep.

I put my stuffed animals on the carpet in front of the window, and spread them out just enough for me to lasso one without knocking all of them over. Once I set them up, I walk back to my bed and twirl my rope high in the air. I get a good loop going and throw it toward the sheep.

Missed.

I get another good loop going. This time I aim for the longhorn.

"Yee-haw!"

Missed again.

Firecrackers!

I think I know why my luck isn't very good tonight. I really don't like Dad calling Macey baby girl. And why didn't Mom and Dad give me a job at the store? I'm sure there's something I could do.

Dad's voice rings through my door. "Mya, stop the lassoing. Nugget, turn off the video games. It's time for dinner."

Holy moly, Dad's got excellent hearing. How can you hear a lasso? Maybe he heard me when I yelled "Yee-haw!" I drop my rope and *ka-clunk* past my bed. Nugget's door and mine open at the same time. We race down the hall, elbowing each other for first place, blocking each other on the steps with our arms. Finally I beat him by one step.

"You cheated, Mya."

"You lost, Nugget."

"Only because you cheated," he says.

"You sound like a loser who got dusted by his younger sister," I say.

He nudges me out of his way. We're too close to the dining-room table for me to nudge him back.

Dad's looking our way. I'd get busted for sure.

Dinner's good, but I can't wait for family time. As soon as he's finished, Dad wipes his mouth, gets up from the table, and says, "I'll be right back."

Mom shrugs, and so does Nugget. Where did he go? Does he have a surprise for us? I love surprises! I'm still grinning until he comes back to the dining room with the *Bluebonnet Tribune* and his laptop. I watch him plug in his computer and turn it on. Mom frowns.

"Darrell, what are you doing?"

"I'm trying to find out if there was a change in corn prices since I read about them this morning in the newspaper. All of us feed-store owners have been talking about it today."

Mom's still frowning. "Honey, please don't start that bad habit of bringing electronics to the table. This is family time."

Dad's eyes appear above the top of his computer. His eyebrows are close together, and by the sound of his voice, he doesn't want to talk about this. "Monica, I need to know what's going on around here. This won't take long."

Mom separates her words as she talks. Even though she doesn't get louder, the way she says those words makes you focus, and she has all of our attention.

"Well, if you want to know what's going on around here, why don't you open your eyes and look around the house! I haven't had a chance to fold clothes, vacuum the floor, wash dishes, or anything like that because Macey needed all my attention today. She demanded it! Every time I put her down, she screamed. I thought if I let her holler for a few minutes, she'd scream herself to sleep. But she didn't. That's what's going on around here. I could use some help, Darrell, instead of you looking for corn prices—something you can't do a thing about. And anyway, this is supposed to be family time!"

Silence.

Dad closes the laptop, stacks his newspaper on top of it, and stares at Mom. She stares back. I swing my feet under the table and lower my face closer to my plate so I can't see them. But across the table, I can see my brother's fingers drumming the table over and over again. I can't stand it. I have to speak up.

"Do you know what you need, Dad? A newspaper with nothing but good news!"

Nugget stops drumming and looks over at Dad.

Mom nods. "A newspaper with nothing but good news doesn't exist."

Dad turns to Nugget. "You got that inventory list finished?"

Nugget pulls a paper out of his back pocket. "Here's a copy, and I sent one to your email. I think I've figured out how to save the store a hundred fifty dollars a month on supplies."

Dad grins and fist-bumps Nugget. "That's what I'm talking about! I don't know what I'd do without you, boy. That's a special gift, knowing numbers the way you do. I sure appreciate your help."

Nugget smiles. "Sure, Dad. No big deal."

What's going on? I know Dad heard me. He's got excellent hearing. A newspaper with nothing but good news is a wonderful idea. Why did he ignore me?

*"Waaaaaaah! Waaaaaaaaaaaaaaah!"*

Mom reaches into the playpen and gets Macey. "Two shots at the doctor's office."

Dad grins and takes her from Mom. "Hi, Macey. Did that big mean doctor try to hurt my baby girl? Mmm, you smell like baby lotion."

Oh no. It wasn't an accident. He didn't make a mistake. He called her baby girl. Again.

Heat rises in me from my toes to my braids. I take a huge gulp of iced tea, hoping I can feel better after drinking something cold. I wonder how long it's going to take me to realize that I'm no longer his baby girl.

Mom clears her throat. "I have an announcement to make. I got a call from the church today, and they want Macey to be one of the Bluebonnet flower babies during the big birthday party for our town next month. I need to make her a bluebonnet flower costume. The church is creating an area that looks like a garden, and all the Bluebonnet babies will be in it for us to take pictures. She's going to look adorable."

Mom's right. Macey will be a beautiful flower at our town's birthday party. I can imagine her in a gorgeous blue outfit with a bonnet on her head. I look over at Dad. He's smiling at Macey. Did he look at me like that when I was her age? He gets up with Macey in his arms and winks at Mom.

"Sounds like fun," he says.

This feels like the perfect time to talk about what's going on in my class. I jump into the conversation. "So today, Mrs. Davis gave each of us ten thousand dollars."

I look around the table to see who's going to be the first person to ask me why in the why Mrs. Davis would give her class that kind of money.

Instead Nugget turns to Dad.

"The Rockets and the Spurs battle it out in the west. Game starts in ten."

Dad nods at Nugget. "Son, help your mom take these dishes to the kitchen, and then join me in the living room. That's exactly what I need to relax my mind. A good ball game."

Mom lets out a big sigh, scoots back from the table, and begins to collect our plates. Nugget helps her as he talks about a new company where inventory supplies are cheaper. When the last dish is taken, I'm still sitting at the table, alone, wondering if I'm all of sudden invisible. Mom and Nugget went one way. Dad and Macey went the other way. No one asked me for help.

What's happening? I thought we were going to have family time. It's all Nugget's fault. I was talking when he interrupted me. Why didn't Mom tell him to wait his turn? Why didn't Macey start crying? I would have totally known she was crying because she knew what Nugget did to me was wrong. Mom, Macey, and I are supposed to stick together. After all, we're cowgirls.

Maybe this corn-price thing is more important to Dad than I thought. I want to help him smile and be happy again. I make good grades and I don't get in trouble at school, so I'm already helping there. I keep my room clean. That's not it. Maybe if I hide the *Bluebonnet Tribune* so Dad can't find it! That might work one or two times, but then he'd figure things out.

I still think a heap of good news would make Dad smile. I bet he's worried about corn prices the same way I'm worried about the kind of business I'm going to start. Maybe I'll just look for good news to write down. Then I'll talk about it at dinner during family time!

That may actually help both of us, because if we're smiling, we're not worrying!

It's important that I make a really good grade in economics, because I like it. But Dad is so much more important than that.

And I'm going to prove it.

## Chapter Five

Tuesday morning, I shove both feet into my favorite pink cowgirl boots, slide both arms through my brown vest to wear over my white blouse, and then ease a small notepad into the back pocket of my jeans. I've got a pencil in my hand in case I see something that looks like good news. Downstairs, I practice by writing about Macey laughing out loud and hearing her baby talk all morning while Mom braided my hair.

On my way to school, I jot down notes about the awesome weather and the birds chirping as they gather on the telephone wires. And in the Cave, I listen to music. When DJ Cool Breezy names the number-one song, I write it down so Dad will know, too.

When the bell rings, I ease my notepad back into my pocket and join my classmates as we rush to our seats so we won't be counted as late. After the Pledge of Allegiance and moment of silence, Mrs. Davis has a stack of papers in her hands. "Please take one of these and pass the rest to the person behind you. This is a form used to create a business plan. I need everything filled out and handed back to me by Friday."

I take the stack of forms from Michael, who sits in front of me, get one, and pass the rest on to Kenyan. The more I read, the wider my eyes get!

## THE NEW BUSINESSES OF BLUEBONNET

1. NAME OF BUSINESS _____
2. OWNER(S) _____
3. TYPE OF BUSINESS _____
4. HOW WILL YOU MARKET YOUR BUSINESS? (SHOW PROOF BY FRIDAY) _____
5. HOW MUCH WILL IT COST TO OPEN YOUR BUSINESS FOR ONE DAY? $_____

6. WHAT SUPPLIES WILL YOU NEED, AND
   HOW MUCH WILL THEY COST, FOR YOUR
   BUSINESS TO STAY OPEN A FULL YEAR?
   (MAKE A LIST)

_____

_____

_____

_____

_____

Mrs. Davis talks as she walks. "Class, think hard about the supplies you will need to purchase with your real money, and be realistic. Use your real funds to answer number five on the business plan. Use your Monopoly money to answer number six on the business plan. Any questions?"

I fold the paper and tuck it inside my left boot, take out my notepad, and write down all of the information. I can't wait to tell my parents about this! My family already owns a business, so I know how to answer these questions. I can see myself opening up a line-dancing club. Yee-haw! To the left, to the left, to the right, to the right, then kick and stomp, kick and stomp, and ride that pony, ride!

But best of all, this will be good news that I can share with Dad tonight so he won't be so mad at the table and we can have more family time.

At recess, all my classmates talk about the businesses they plan to open. I overhear Kenyan and David bragging about their skills.

"My homemade chocolate-chip cookies are boo-yang, and I can make at least five dozen for twenty-five bucks," says Kenyan. "Family, neighbors, friends, everybody wants them for holidays and birthdays. I'm going to call my business Cookies from Kenyan."

David fist-bumps him. "Almost everybody loves chocolate-chip cookies. But after eating all that sugar in your cookies, people will need to exercise."

Kenyan fist-bumps David. "We're going to be famous! I'll bring in a batch, let everybody *oooh* and *aaah* over how good they are. And then I'll start charging for them. Twenty-five cents a cookie! What about you, David? You're going to start an exercise class?"

David busts a few moves in front of Kenyan, to show off his skills. "No way! I'm going to give dance lessons. It's going to be called Dancing with David. It won't cost me anything since I've aleady got the music downloaded on my cell phone."

Kenyan gives David a high five. "That's going to be awesome!"

Good gravy. I was thinking about opening up a line-dancing club, but David's a much better dancer than me.

Kenyan chuckles. "After me, you're probably the best dancer in the class."

David laughs. "You wish! I'm the best dancer on the planet! I can't decide if I want to open a real studio, you know, like at recess, or somewhere else."

"I bet you get an A either way, bro," says Kenyan.

I jump when I hear my name.

"Hi, Mya."

"Hello, Mya."

It's the twins.

"Oh, hey!" I say. "What's going on?"

They both giggle. "You know what's going on," says Skye.

"You know what's going on," says Starr.

"Our new businesses," says Skye.

"Talking about our new business," says Starr.

I smile. "I knew that. Have you decided?"

"Oh yes. It's called Two Knew You," says Skye.

"You'll love Two Knew You," says Starr.

"We believe everyone has been on this earth several times before," says Skye.

"People are recyclable, too," says Starr.

"Starr and I are going to tell people what they

were in their past life, where they lived, all that good stuff. We've already got a crystal ball, so we'll buy two fortune-teller hats and that's it," says Skye.

"That's it! We'll make a gajillion dollars," says Starr.

"Our business will explain lots of people's questions . . . like 'I was at this restaurant last week, and I felt like I had been there before.' Well, they probably had been there, but maybe back then, they were a chair, or a menu! Get it?" asks Starr.

"You understand, don't you?" asks Skye.

"Of course I do," I say.

"We've got another big surprise, too," says Skye.

"A big surprise," says Starr.

"What about you, Mya?" asks Skye.

"Have you decided yet?" asks Starr.

I shake my head, wishing I could hear an idea rattling around in there. As much as I'd like to do something with horses, or on a ranch, I couldn't even get a used horseshoe for twenty-five bucks. I'd thought about opening up a chili restaurant since Mom showed me how to make it a few months ago, but that would mean I'd be stuck in the kitchen every night cooking. I'm trying to think when I hear a familiar voice.

"What kind of business are you opening? Like I

really care," says Naomi.

Even with the smart-aleck words, she didn't say it in a mean way, so I decide not to answer in a mean way. After all, there was a time when Naomi was my best friend.

"I don't know. I'm still working on that. What about you? Not that I care or anything," I say, just to match her.

Naomi grins, and her teeth are so white and bright that I need sunglasses. "I'm opening up a party-planning business. My mother is a professional party planner, and I've helped her with so many weddings, parties, even funerals, that I'm practically a professional already. I've already got my first clients."

I can't believe it. "Who?"

Only one side of her mouth grins. "The twins!"

"That's our other big surprise," says Skye.

"Surprise!" says Starr.

Naomi continues. "It makes perfect sense for me to plan their birthday party. I mean, we've been friends since forever. I may have been the first friend they had when they moved here. Doesn't that make sense to you? And April Fool's Day is on a Friday this year! Perfect!"

I'm so angry I can't talk. That's a hands-down,

no-good, double-Dutch lie.

Naomi puts one hand on her hip as the other twirls her hair. "And guess what? I called Mom. She got DJ Cool Breezy to come. He's always DJing parties where everybody wears black and white. I'm going to do the same for Starr and Skye! I'm actually spreading the word right now at recess. Everybody will have to wear black and white to represent stars against the night sky, get it? Like Starr and Skye! Can you say party of the year?"

Naomi and the twins walk away but Naomi keeps her eyes on me. "Hurry up and pick a business before all the good ones are gone. You're gonna get stuck with something nobody cares about. Here comes your best friend, Mya. Tell her what I told you."

Connie walks up. Both of us watch Naomi and the twins stop and talk to other boys and girls in our class.

"What did Naomi want?" asks Connie.

I shrug. "Well, she thinks she was friends with the twins before me. She also wanted to know what kind of business I was going to choose. She told me she was doing party planning, and get this—she got DJ Cool Breezy for the twins' party, and she's making everyone wear black and white."

Connie's eyes widen. "What? DJ Cool Breezy? No

way. He is boo-yang cute."

I nod. "Boo-yang. Then she told me I'd better hurry and make a decision before all the good businesses are gone. But you know what she didn't do? She didn't call me Mya Tibbs Fibs."

"She must've fallen and hit that pointy head of hers," says Connie.

I stare at the ground, looking for an answer. "I wonder what she's up to."

## Chapter Six

It's a long walk home as Connie and I talk about the business plan. Neither one of us seems to have good ideas. I nudge her.

"You haven't said much about that picture you're supposed to paint for the Bluebonnet party at the park. Have you started on it yet?"

"I've got nothin'. I need some inspiration, and I don't have it. I mean, I like living here, but drawing a picture about it is a lot different. And I'm not going to draw a boring field of bluebonnet flowers. That would be so lame."

We're walking a few steps ahead of Nugget and

his best friend, Fish. Fish's real name is Homer Leatherwood, because his dad is a big-time baseball fan. But when he was around seven years old, Homer started looking like a blowfish. His big blue eyes make me dizzy because there is too much of those blue eyeballs showing under his eyelids. Kind of like bright lights on a car, only on a fish instead. The name stuck, and he doesn't seem to mind.

They high-five before Fish turns to me with a big smile.

"Hiya, Mya Papaya."

He says that to me every time he sees me, but I never get tired of hearing it. It's not a good cowgirl name like Annie Oakley or Cowgirl Claire, but I like it.

"Where were you this morning? You didn't walk to school with us," I ask.

"Dentist appointment, so I didn't get to tell you Happy Melba Toast Day."

Fish has a calendar of weird holidays like Pickle Day, Boot Day, and hundreds more that I can't even think of. Every morning Nugget and I hear about what's being celebrated.

I frown as I try to think. "Who is she?"

He shrugs. "I guess a lady who makes toast so good that they named it after her."

"If that lady can become famous with toast, maybe I can open an art gallery with nothing but skull art," says Connie.

The business plan folded up inside my boot is making my ankle itch. I don't want to take it out, because then it will remind me of all those blanks on that business form I need to fill in before Friday.

"I don't know what to do. I guess I could open up a jewelry-making store, but I wanted to be the first jewelry-making, calf-roping cowgirl in Bluebonnet. I wanted my store in the front, and my horse tied up in the back," I say.

"Mrs. Davis said be realistic, and that's not realistic, Mya," says Connie.

"I know, but if she had given us real money yesterday, I could've bought that horse."

Nugget gives me a little shove. "Mrs. Davis pulled the old money switcheroo on you guys? I remember she told us she had ten grand for each of us. I almost peed my pants."

Fish, Connie, and I giggle, but then the conversation goes cold. Soon Connie and Fish go their way, while Nugget unlocks the door for us to go inside our house. It looks the same way it did yesterday, so I go upstairs to my room and think about tonight.

I've got a bunch of good news to share during

family time. I'll talk about Connie getting asked by some really important people to paint a picture that looks like life in Bluebonnet. And after recess, I saw a sales paper from Marco's Grocery on Mrs. Davis's desk. Marco's has peas on sale. Since the price of corn is still high, maybe Dad can add peas to his special cattle mix instead of corn. Or maybe he can add toast! That will lead me into Miss Melba Toast Day.

And then I'll end it with Mrs. Davis giving us ten thousand dollars, and how it turned out to be Monopoly money. I tried to tell them yesterday, but no one was paying attention.

Mom and Dad need to laugh. I hate it when they argue, like they did last night when Dad brought his computer to the table. It's hard to have family night after Mom and Dad argue, but if I can make them think about good things, they'll stop arguing.

Maybe that's my job in this family. Macey's job is to be cute. Nugget's job is to be smart. I'm here to report good news and keep the family happy! And if I do my job as well as Macey and Nugget do theirs, Mom and Dad will relax and smile again.

I put my notes in order, do my homework, and wait for Dad to call me for dinner. When he does, I'm so excited that I give him the biggest hug I can and then sit down to eat. As soon as I'm finished, I tell my parents what I've been waiting to say all day.

"Dad, there's no need to bring the laptop to the table. We need to have family night because I've got a whole lot of stuff to talk about. I don't have any news about corn prices, but I do have some good info on peas."

Mom smiles. Dad winks at me. "Okay, let's hear it," he says as he gets Macey out of her playpen.

I stand up and look around the table as if I'm giving a report in school. "Macey giggled the entire time Mom braided my hair. She was in a happy mood. The weather started off a little cooler than yesterday, but not cold enough for a winter coat. Spring is here, and hopefully it is here to stay."

"I hope so, too," says Mom.

Dad holds up a finger. "Amen to that."

Yes! That was good. I'll keep talking like a news reporter since they seem to like that.

"In other news today, my best friend, Connie Tate, has been asked by the city of Bluebonnet to paint a picture that reflects life in Bluebonnet. She is very honored and excited, and Mrs. Davis gave us a new project. Each student in my class has to start their own business."

Nugget interrupts me. "Hey, Dad, remember last

year when Fish and I did the Fish Nugget Firm? We were on fire! Our business was awesome."

Dad nods. "I got two calls from teachers at your school, asking if you could separate their receipts for them again for tax season. I told them you were too busy doing mine!"

Mom and Nugget laugh. I shoot Nugget an ugly frown, but he keeps laughing with Dad. I wait for everyone to stop laughing before I finish.

"And the last bit of good news is, today is Miss Melba Toast's Day. So, let's have a toast for Miss Toast!"

I raise my glass of iced tea and wait. Mom and Dad cover their mouths as if trying to hide another laugh. I think they're laughing about the little joke I made about a toast for Miss Toast. Nugget doesn't roll his eyes, but his face has a whole lot of know-it-all on it, and I can tell he's getting ready to crush me. He looks at Mom and Dad as he talks. "Melba toast isn't a person. Melba toast is . . . a cracker!"

My heart thumps anger. Here he goes again, stealing my time, interrupting me. I side-eye him. "How do you know? She could be a real person."

Nugget looks Dad's way and gives an answer I hadn't heard of. "There was an actress or a singer in Australia named Melba, but she got sick. She had her own chef, and he made her some toast to try to help her feel better. That's where melba toast comes from. If you're going to be a reporter, make sure the news is accurate."

"How did you know that, Nugget?" asks Mom.

"Because Mya is right about one thing. There is a National Melba Toast Day. When Fish mentioned it, as soon as I got home I went online to research melba toast and found the same answer about the Australian woman's chef in three different places. But the bigger issue is National Melba Toast Day is tomorrow. Fish must've looked at the wrong day. Melba Toast is always celebrated on March twenty-third. That's why you've got to do your research, Mya, and not rely on what other people say. Fish was a whole day off."

I don't say anything else. I'm scared to, because I didn't do any research on Miss Melba, and I don't want to dig a deeper hole for myself.

"I'd never heard that story," said Dad with a grin. "Mya, maybe you should check with Nugget before you report your news, to make sure it's accurate."

I would rather Dad drop a bag of bricks on my head than say that. I glance at my brother. He's got that "I'm smarter than you" grin on his face. All I can do is frown.

"Mmm, I love how Macey smells," says Dad. He closes his eyes and holds her close.

Macey coos, and both my parents go bananas. Mom pulls up a chair near Dad, and they sniff at her like she's made of candy.

Nugget scoots back. "I'll clear the table off expeditiously for you, Mom."

She smiles. "Thanks, Nugget. I need to cut out this pattern for Macey's bluebonnet costume. It shouldn't take me too long to get it done."

Clearing the table is my job. Now Nugget's trying to take over. Well, I've got something for him, and he's not going to like it at all! Tomorrow night I'm going to sound so smart when I talk to Mom and Dad that Nugget's going to think I've been taking college courses!

Why didn't I think of this before? I'm supposed to be a mix of my younger sister and older brother. It seems as if I have to be smart like Nugget and smell like Macey.

So if being super smart or super smelly is what makes a kid special in this house, then that's exactly what they're going to get. Tomorrow night after dinner, when I'm giving Dad his good-news report,

I'll use big words just like my brother does.

Maybe I'll use a word Nugget's never heard of. Yeah! Then he'll know how I feel all the time. And after two or three coats of baby lotion on my skin, it should be super soft and smelling so awesome that Dad will close his eyes and say, "Mmmm, Mya smells good!"

I grin while thinking about it.

"What's so funny?" asks Nugget.

I give him a stink eye and hope he can smell it as I wrinkle my lips like the words coming up taste bad. "Oh, just wishing I had a cracker."

I hope he gets the message that I didn't appreciate him interrupting me with that Melba story. But it doesn't matter. Tomorrow, he's the one who's going to be toast.

# Chapter Seven

Today is Wednesday. I call it hump day because it reminds me of riding a wild stallion like a real cowgirl! Yee-haw! And when the three o'clock bell rings, I realize Mrs. Davis didn't give any homework. With everything I'm going through with Mom and Dad, and having to figure out a business to start, I really needed a no-homework day. I rush into the Cave, get my backpack from my cabinet, and boot-scoot out of there.

Right now, all I want to do is see Macey. There's something about being around my baby sister that makes me feel better. When I hold her, I feel calm, and nothing else in the world matters. It's not her fault that Dad doesn't call me baby girl anymore. It's not her fault that we haven't had family time at the table this week. But that doesn't mean I can't have special time with her.

When she looks at me, her legs kick like she's swimming in her crib. They keep kicking, even when I pick her up. That's how I know she's glad to see me. Right now, she may be the only person in the family who really sees me. And that's why I'm rushing home.

I don't wait on Nugget. I could get in trouble for that. We're not supposed to leave each other on our way to school or when we walk home. This will be the second time I've done it.

Firecrackers! Nugget has the key. I'm about to ring the doorbell when I hear my brother call my name.

"I'm coming," he says, jogging toward the house.

As he steps up to the door, he gives me a long glare. I know why, but I don't care. If he's going to be a tattletale, let him. He turns the key in the lock and heads upstairs.

I tiptoe down the hall and poke my head into Macey's room. She's sprawled out in the crib, asleep. Mom's asleep, too, but she's in her own room. I grin, because seeing Macey makes me smile—but if I'm not careful, I'll wake her, and Mom may get mad at me. I turn to leave, and that's when I see something that reminds me of my plan.

The baby lotion.

I look over my shoulder to be sure Mom's not watching, grab the big bottle of baby lotion, and stick it in my boot. As fast and quiet as I can, I tiptoe out and go upstairs. When I see Nugget shut his door, I shut mine, too, and lock it. There's no way I want him to see what I'm doing or ask me any questions. I turn on my computer and Google "big words."

I find my words and study them. And I've decided that I'm going to try my news reporting idea again. It was actually working well last night. Dad was smiling. Mom was really into what I was saying. And then that chicken-headed brother of mine interrupted.

I'm not going to let that happen again. Tonight is my night, and I'm going to be the best good-news-reportin', baby-lotion-smellin', big-word-usin' person at the dinner table!

Dad should be home by now. That leaves me with only a few minutes to get ready.

I wash up in my bathroom, even use soap, to

make sure I don't have any school smells on me. Sometimes I can get sweaty after recess, or accidentally spill something on my blouse from lunch. Mom sometimes tells me I smell like "outside." I don't see what's wrong with that, but to her, that's not good. So I wash with extra soap so I'll have a clean start.

As I put on the first coat of baby lotion, I go over my big words, using them in sentences. I even practice looking as if using those words is no big deal. The second coat feels slicker than the first. Maybe because I've already got some on. Mom usually puts one coat on Macey, but my little sister is so much smaller than me. I'm sure I need at least three.

Dad hollers up to me. "Mya, you have company!"

What? I'm not expecting anyone. Maybe it's Connie.

I squirt on the last coat of lotion, and then pinch my cheeks to make them rosy. I grab my good-news report for Dad and open my bedroom door. Nugget walks by and slows down.

"Is Macey in your room?"

"Definitely not" is all I say as I pass him on my way to the steps.

"Smells like it," he says behind me.

I'm surprised when I see the twins standing in front of the sofa, each holding a pink box.

"Hey, Mya, we came to see Macey," says Skye.

"We're here to celebrate her birthday," says Starr.

My head tilts to the side. "Her birthday is in October."

"Yeah, but her half-year birthday is coming up! Let's party!" says Skye.

"Time to party with Macey!" says Starr.

I smile and lead the way to the nursery.

"You wear the same lotion as Macey? I can smell it," say Skye.

"I can totally smell it," says Starr.

I've got this lotion on for a special reason. I want Dad to notice me. But that's not for the twins to know. As I'm about to say something, Skye lets me off the hook.

"Starr and I wear the same lotion, too. It's a sister thing. I get it, Mya."

"We totally get it," says Starr.

Inside Macey's room, Mom's rocking her, but Macey is wide-awake.

Mom gives the twins a big smile. "Well, look who's come to visit!"

"Good afternoon, Mrs. Tibbs. We came to see Macey," says Skye.

"Good afternoon, Mrs. Tibbs," says Starr.

Mom puts Macey in her crib, and she begins to coo, and the twins love it.

"Mya, dinner will be ready in thirty minutes. The twins are welcome to stay," says Mom.

I don't want the twins to stay for dinner. I've got business to handle with Dad and Nugget. And some things shouldn't be seen by people outside the family.

The twins look around the room and smile.

"I remember decorating this room before Mrs. Tibbs downloaded Macey," says Skye.

"I do, too," says Starr.

They point to the wall they decorated.

"Those twins, Sears and Macey. We did an awesome job painting them, Starr."

"An awesome job," says Starr.

"Yes, and we're never going to paint over them," I say.

The twins hug, as if I've told them they won a million dollars. When they let go of each other, their expressions change.

"Let's get this party started!" says Skye.

Starr opens up her box and takes out four party hats and four party favors that make noise. I blow on mine, and it sound like a goose. Macey laughs. Starr and Skye blow on theirs. Macey laughs again.

I turn on a radio, and the three of us dance in a circle in front of Macey's bed, blowing on these party favors and watching Macey, in her birthday-party hat, enjoy it.

Finally Skye stops. "I almost forgot about her gift."

"We can't forget to give her the gift," says Starr.

"Here, you open it for her, Mya," says Skye.

"You're her sister. You do it," says Starr.

I open up the pink box and take out a little dancing ballerina made of porcelain.

"This ballerina looks exactly like Macey," I say.

"Every girl should dance," says Skye.

"We love to dance," says Starr.

It feels good to have friends like the twins. I hope we're friends forever. I'd do anything for them, and I know they'd do the same for me.

"Mya, it's time for dinner," yells Mom.

"Would you like to stay for dinner?" I ask.

"No, we can't. Dad's waiting outside in the van," says Skye.

"We have to go," says Starr.

My eyebrows scrunch together. "He's been out there this whole time?"

"No, he just got here," says Skye.

"Just got here," says Starr.

There was a time when I would've asked how he knew it was time to pick them up. But so many weird and strange things go on in the twins' lives that I've learned to accept them.

"Okay, well, thanks for coming over and hanging out with Macey and me. It was fun."

Macey coos, and they coo back to her. I walk the twins to the front door.

"See you tomorrow at school," I say.

"Definitely," says Skye.

"Most definitely," says Starr.

I wave to their dad, say goodbye, and walk to the dining room. I'm glad the twins are my friends. There's no way Naomi and her family are better or closer friends with them than me and my family.

And I think the twins just proved it.

# Chapter Eight

Mom, Dad, and Nugget are already in the dining room when I get there. With a happy face, I walk over to Dad with lots of energy and hug him.

"Hi."

He hugs me back. "Mmm—you smell like Macey."

I keep hugging him as the grin on my face stretches toward my ears. "Thanks. I've got some great things to talk about during family time."

He winks at me. "Sounds good. Oh, and happy Melba Toast Day, right?"

Nugget snorts, and Dad chuckles with him. I cut my eyes at my brother and keep talking to Dad.

"Most of the information in my good-news report tonight is alfresco."

Nugget jerks his head my way. "Alfresco? Isn't that a drink?"

I give him the melba toast look he gave me yesterday.

"No. Alfresco means outside. Most of my good news has to do with the outdoors."

"Where'd you learn that word?" he asks.

I don't answer because I've got a bunch of those big words, locked and loaded in my brain. I plan to fire them like cannonballs until Nugget learns to keep his big fat mouth closed when I'm talking. I want him to feel how I felt last night.

Of course I hope Mom and Dad are impressed with the way I smell and the way I talk, but tonight, I declare a word war on my brother, and he's going down.

Mom's made soup and salad for dinner. It's quick to eat, and that's what I need tonight.

Nugget takes a huge gulp of his sweet tea and sets it down on the table.

"I got another A on my science test today. That makes four As in a row.'

Before Mom and Dad congratulate him, I give Nugget a taste of what he's done to me.

"I'm sure there are other ways to obtain accolades than through gasconading."

Mom stabs some of her salad. "Gasconading. That's a good word."

Dad stops drinking in the middle of a big gulp. I can tell Nugget's Googling his brain for a definition. Finally, he gives up.

"What's gasconading?" he asks.

My eyes zone in on his. "You look bumfuzzled."

Nugget frowns. "What did you call me?"

"Gasconading is bragging. Bumfuzzled is confused." I lean across the table. "You're not the only sesqui . . . sesquimedalian in this house."

Nugget leans toward me. "The word is sesquipedalian, and I *do* know what that means."

"Wow, Mya, you sure are using some big words today," says Dad.

"Some of them I've never heard of," says Mom.

Nugget frowns at me. "She's trying to be like me."

"A gasconader? I don't think so," I say, and cross my arms.

"Trust me, Mya, you don't want to get into a big-word contest with me," says Nugget.

Mom holds up her glass and shakes the ice in it. "I don't have a problem with Mya expanding her vocabulary. As a matter of fact, I think that's wonderful. But Mya, what I do have a problem with is how you smell. Where did you get that baby lotion?"

"Macey's room."

Mom looks mad. "Why are you wearing your sister's lotion?"

"I guess because . . ." I look over at Dad. He seems to be waiting on my answer, so I say what I know he'd say. "Because I like how it smells."

"I can't blame her for that," says Dad. "As a matter of fact, where is Macey?"

"She's in her crib, but Mya, please don't put any more of Macey's lotion on. Number one, it's expensive, and two, that lotion is for babies. I bought you your own."

"Yes, ma'am."

I can't bear to look at Dad or Mom. They're the reason I smeared that stuff all over me in the first place. I had to get their attention somehow so they would listen to my good news. I just knew big words and Macey's lotion would do the trick. I knew it worked because Dad hugged me so tight today that it made me smile and close my eyes. I bet he was smiling, too.

"I'm going to get Macey and then watch something on ESPN," he says.

I fight back tears. "But what about my good-news report?"

Dad snaps his fingers. "Tell you what. Save it for me. Maybe your Wednesday news is going to be the perfect Thursday news for me, okay?"

"Sure," I say, biting my lip and ordering my tears to stay in my eyes.

Nugget's looking at me. His eyes seem sad. Maybe he's realizing what a dirty rotten brother he's been. I'm about to get up from the table when Mom surprises me.

"You know, Mya, I was looking forward to hearing you read from your good-news newspaper. I guess that means I'll get to hear a double one tomorrow, right?"

"Yes, ma'am," I say.

She gets up from the table. "I've got to work on Macey's flower outfit for the party."

I leave Nugget at the table, go to my room, and lock the door. The first thing I destroy is that dumb good-news report. I wad it up as tightly as I can. What was I thinking?

In order for me to keep Dad's attention, I'd have to create a whole newspaper full of good news from all over Bluebonnet. There would have to be advertisements and articles and funny stuff, and of course I'd put stuff in there about—

Wait a minute.

I open my bedroom door, rush downstairs, and grab the phone. There's only one person I want to share this idea with.

"Hello, Connie?"

"Hi, Mya, what's up?"

"I'm going to start a newspaper!"

"That's a really, really good idea."

"I know. But I want you to be my partner. You can take all of the photos."

"This is sounding better by the minute," says Connie.

"We could go around the neighborhood and ask people if they have any good news."

Connie agrees. "That's another great idea. And it will make people want to get a copy of our newspaper. Are you going to charge money for it?"

I stop. Holy moly. I hadn't even thought about that.

"Think about it, Connie. If you tried to open an art gallery, I bet you would end up getting a loan from Mrs. Davis because ten thousand dollars wouldn't be enough money."

"Aha! But if we put our money together . . . I see where you're going with this."

"We wouldn't have to get a loan. I bet twenty thousand dollars could start a newspaper business for us! And think of all the money we could make! I'm thinking millions of dollars!"

"Slow down, cowgirl. We haven't even made the first newspaper yet. Okay, what else can we do besides talk to our neighbors?"

"What about all the things going on in our town? With Bluebonnet's birthday party coming up, that would be huge! And then you can draw as many pictures as you want and put them in the paper! And what if places like the Burger Bar or my dad's store are having a buy one, get one free sale? I could put that in the paper, too."

Connie nods. "That's good thinking. Do we want anything in there about our school?"

I sit on the bed. "Of course! We have to put stuff in there about school."

"I think it'd be fun if you put some of those silly taradiddles in the paper."

"Wait a minute, Connie. . . . What if we named the newspaper the *Taradiddle*?"

Connie's voice gets louder. "No, how about the *Texas Taradiddle*?"

"Jambalaya! That's it! The *Texas Taradiddle*!"

"Mya, I've got the best idea for marketing. We

can charge our classmates twenty-five dollars of their Monopoly money, and they can advertise in our newspaper! They can write that down as their marketing idea!"

"And we can say our marketing idea was allowing the businesses in our classroom, and around Bluebonnet, to advertise in our newspaper!"

"Yes! That's perfect! We're going to get an A!"

For Connie, it's all about getting an A. But for me, I found the one thing that will get Mom and Dad to see me as special without talking, acting, or smelling like Nugget or Macey.

I stop pacing and grab my rope from the hook on the wall. I need to do some thinking.

"Okay, let's talk more tomorrow. Bye, Connie."

Once my stuffed animals are set up, I twirl my rope and throw for the sheep.

Missed.

Seems like I'm missing at everything. Hopefully this newspaper will make Mom and Dad see that I can be special at something, too. But I better make sure I don't miss.

# Chapter Nine

On Thursday morning, I'm up before the alarm goes off. I slide my closet door to the left and stare at the clothes hanging inside. I'm looking for one thing, and one thing only.

There it is.

I reach for my blue fedora hat with the black ribbon around it, parked next to my cowgirl hat on the shelf. I got that hat for Christmas last year from my grandma, the same one who gave me my jewelry-making kit. I've never worn the fedora, but it's the perfect hat for a reporter.

I get dressed and head downstairs to watch the

morning news. I want to see a reporter in action, to make sure I've got everything down. I make my eyebrows go up and down like the lady on the television. I smile and pretend I'm holding a microphone as someone speaks. I nod my head yes, to agree with the person talking.

No problem. I got this.

"Mya, I'm ready to do your hair," yells Mom.

I take off my fedora and head to my chair.

"Only one braid this morning, please," I say.

"Okay," she replies.

My ears wait for any signs of a conversation from her. When she stays quiet, I talk to her.

"Starr and Skye are having a birthday party at school, in the Cave. Isn't that cool?"

"Uh-huh," grunts Mom.

*Oh no. Not again. I'll try something different.*

"I took your advice! I'm starting a newspaper. And here's my cool reporter's hat."

"Uh-huh," says Mom again as she brushes the edges of my hair.

"It's going to be awesome."

"Uh-huh." I feel her separate my hair into four bunches, and I stop her.

"I only wanted one braid, Mom."

"Oh, I'm sorry. My mind was somewhere else.

I'm making four. Is that okay?"

"Sure," I say. One braid each for Mom, Dad, Nugget, and Macey. I'm left out again.

It's not a good feeling, but I don't know what to do about it, so once she finishes, I get my backpack, put on my fedora, and head toward the door. I don't know where my brother is, and I haven't seen Dad all morning. I don't care. I'll walk to school by myself.

I'm waiting on the light to change so I can cross the street when Nugget catches up with me. "It was really nice of you to leave without me, Mya."

"It's not my fault you woke up late."

"I didn't wake up late. I've been in Dad's study helping him with this corn issue."

The bubbles in my guts rise all the way up to my throat, and they're forming words that I can't keep in my mouth. "Well, if you're having such a wonderful time with Dad this morning, why didn't he drive you to school!"

"What? He's not going to drive me to school. What's your drama?"

I stop and let him have it. "What's *your* drama!

He stops, too, and frowns. "Why would you even ask me that?"

"Because you're always correcting me or trying

to one-up me in front of Mom and Dad."

"I could say the same about you. I mean, what's the deal with the big words last night and the baby lotion? You trying to make them think you're better than me and Macey?"

"I'd never do that," I say, and turn to walk away.

Nugget grabs my arm. I pull away from his grip as he talks with a frown.

"Look," he says. "I know Mom and Dad are really stressed right now, with the price of corn going up and trying to take care of Macey. Why don't you give them a break? Whatever you're upset about, drop it. It can't be that important, right?"

I didn't realize how quickly tears could come to my eyes until now. My heart's pounding so hard in my chest that it's forcing the tears out of my eyes.

"What now? Why are you crying? Oh my gosh! I didn't say anything! You are really acting weird," says Nugget. "And why are you wearing that hat and a pencil behind your ear?"

For the first time in as long as I can remember, Nugget doesn't understand what I'm going through. He doesn't get it. He doesn't get me. He doesn't see that what's going on inside me is very important. He doesn't see that it hurts. He just wants me to ignore how I feel!

Hasn't he heard Mom and Dad cut me off at dinner? Hasn't he heard Dad call Macey baby girl? He's the one helping Mom clear the table now. It's as if I'm not important at all. Like there's nothing special about me.

What is wrong with me? It's not Nugget's fault that he's smart. It's not Macey's fault that she's cute. I've got to prove I've got something worth liking.

Mr. Winky's at the front door. He greets Nugget first, and then me. "Well, here comes the best rootin' tootin' cowgirl in Bluebonnet! But today she looks like she means business in that blue hat of hers! Yes, yes, yes, it's going to be a wonderful day at Y.E.S. Yes, it is."

I give Mr. Winky a wimpy wave because that's about all I've got this morning. I *ka-clunk* into my classroom like a cowgirl in a business hat.

"Good morning, Mya. Love the fedora," says Mrs. Davis with a smile.

"Mornin', and thanks, Mrs. Davis," I say back.

"That sure sounded grumpy. Having a tough morning?" she asks.

"I don't want to smile today. I want to let my smile muscles rest."

Mrs. Davis nods. "Okay. But if there is something you'd like to talk about, I'll be more than happy to listen. And even though that fedora is awesome, don't forget you have to take it off before the bell rings."

"Yes, ma'am," I say, heading toward the Cave.

Connie rushes to me as soon as I step inside. "Your hat is so boo-yang! And the pencil behind your ear looks perfect, Mya. I brought my camera to take a few photos, since I know we've got a deadline of . . . like . . . tomorrow. You need to make an announcement! The bell is going to ring in ten minutes!"

I wipe my face, to be sure there're no leftover tears hanging around. And sometimes when I wipe my hand across my face, it acts like a magic wand. It takes away the sad feelings and puts me in a different mood. I hope it works like that now.

I put my hand in the air, and in the loudest whisper I can push out of my mouth, I ask for everyone's attention. I stand in the middle of the Cave thinking there's not a business owner on the planet who needs a perfect business more than me. I bet my classmates are just looking for a good grade for their efforts. So am I, but I also want my parents to recognize how special I am, that I'm capable of helping our family and bringing smiles to them like Macey and Nugget.

I've got Connie to help me. She thinks this is only about our school project and doesn't realize it's much more to me than that. She doesn't need to know. No one does.

It's too personal.

Right now, there's only one thing I have to do, and that's to convince my classmates that they need the *Texas Taradiddle*, even if I'm the only one who knows the whole truth behind it.

# Chapter Ten

Once everyone in the Cave is quiet, I spill the beans.

"Connie and I have decided to start a good-news newspaper."

"Awesome," says Starr.

"Very awesome," says Skye.

"That's different," says Lisa.

"Never heard of a good-news newspaper," says Naomi, rolling her eyes.

"Sounds cool!" says Kenyan.

I give Kenyan a serious look.

"This isn't about being cool. This is about business."

My classmates move closer. My face tightens to a serious expression. "Mrs. Davis is playing hardball with this business project. We need to show her that we can do it."

Heads nod.

David crosses his arms. "What's this all about, Mya?"

I dead-eye David. "Have you finished the marketing part of your business plan?"

"No," he says.

I look over at Lisa. "What about you?"

"Not yet," she says.

"Mary Frances? Are you finished with yours?"

"I'm not even sure what marketing is," she says. "I'm going to get a bad grade."

I *ka-clunk* over to her. "No, you're not. That's because Connie and I are going to take care of you. We're going to take care of all of you!"

Kenyan stuffs his hands in his pockets. "How are you going to do that?"

I've got them right where I want them. "I know everybody in here has looked at a newspaper. What does it have in it? Advertising! Every business that advertises in the newspaper is actually doing their marketing!"

The twins step forward.

"We could advertise in your newspaper," says Skye.

"Totally advertise," says Starr.

"And that would be our marketing," says Skye.

"We'd get an A for marketing," says Starr.

I love the twins. I point at them and grin. "Exactly!"

Michael gets into the conversation. "When will the first edition of your newspaper come out with our marketing in it? Our business plans are due tomorrow."

"We've got you covered. Connie and I will deliver the first edition tomorrow morning. That means we all meet Mrs. Davis's deadline."

"Is marketing free?" asks Johnny.

The room goes quiet. Everyone's staring at me. So I drop the news like it's hot.

"Advertising in my newspaper is going to cost you twenty-five dollars."

Kenyan puts both hands on his head. "Are you crazy? That's all we've got! I don't have that kind of money for marketing."

"Neither do I," says Mary Frances.

"Forget it. You might as well ask for a thousand, because I don't have it," says Michael.

"Yes, you do. We all do," says David.

Heads turn to watch David as he walks to his cabinet, grabs his envelope of Monopoly money, and shuffles back over to me.

"Here's a green twenty and a pink five. This better be worth it."

I take the money, hand it to Connie, and put our reputations on the line. "I'll let you be the judge of that when Connie and I bring copies of the *Texas Taradiddle* to school tomorrow. All you have to do is write down your name and the name of your business on this notepad, and that's it! Congratulations! Your marketing problems are over. Anybody else?"

Several of our classmates dash to their cabinets for a green twenty and a pink five. Connie collects the money while I pass around the notepad. Some of my classmates choose not to advertise with me. That's fine. It's their loss. Connie and I are going to make an A. Last night while I was on the phone with Connie, it took her forever to help me understand why we will do our best marketing by marketing our newspaper to others! My classmates are using my business product because Connie and I marketed it to them! Yee-haw! So far, so good.

The bell's going to ring in thirty seconds. I *ka-clunk* as quickly as I can to my seat. Even though Mrs. Davis knows we're in the Cave, she will count us tardy if we're not seated when the bell rings. I take off my hat and place it at the corner of my desk. As I take a seat, a green twenty and a pink five fall on top of my fedora. I look up. It's Naomi.

"You're supposed to give the money to Connie."

"I'm giving it to you. Don't mess up, Mya. This better be worth it. And why did you take Monopoly money when you could have had real cash?"

"Connie and I put our money together. We've got plenty to open our business for one day. But we need more Monopoly money for the business plan. And I'll tell you like I told David. Tomorrow you can be the judge of whether or not it's worth it."

"Okay, I will," she says, and takes a seat before the bell rings.

Mrs. Davis takes attendance, and we stand for the Pledge of Allegiance and the moment of silence. After that, the morning seems to fly by. When lunch is over, Mrs. Davis lets me go back to our classroom and get my hat so I can wear it on the playground during recess. Connie and I spread the news about our newspaper to the fifth graders. She takes pictures as I interview students. I start with Mary Frances.

"I'm working on my front-page article, and I was thinking it should be really special. And then it came to me that I should ask everybody a question. What makes you special?"

Oh no. That must have been in my conscience. I didn't mean to ask that question, but it's out there now, and I can't take it back. Mary Frances thinks for a moment, and then grins.

"I have my grandma's sky-blue eyes. No one else in my family has them but me."

I write it down. David answers next. "I volunteer at the animal rescue shelter two Saturdays a month. When I get older, I'm going to volunteer even more. I feel really special when I help the animals."

I ask lots of students about what makes them special, and the more I ask, the worse I feel. They're coming up with all kinds of good answers. I didn't know about Mary Frances's grandma's eyes, or David's love for rescue animals. I wish I could belt out a reason why I'm special. But I'm not feeling that way right now. I can't even get my mom to talk to me while she braids my hair.

When it's Skye and Starr's turn, they seem excited about answering.

"People see us as the same," says Skye.

"The same," says Starr.

"And we are the same, but we see each other as special," says Skye.

"Very special," says Starr.

"What makes me feel special is I was born first. I'm the oldest. And as the oldest, I feel a special responsibility to take care of my baby sister."

"I was born last. I'm the youngest. And as the youngest, I feel a special responsibility to take care of my older sister."

They turn toward each other and hug.

"I didn't know you felt that way, Starr," says Skye.

"I totally didn't know you felt that way, Skye," says Starr.

I stop writing to tell them how I see them individually. "Skye, you always sip your milk at lunch. Starr gulps hers."

They giggle, and I keep going. "And this doesn't always happen, but I would say ninety percent of the time Skye speaks first, and then Starr speaks after her."

"That's true," says Skye.

"Ninety percent of the time, that's true," says Starr.

I point at Starr. "Your temper is way worse than Skye's. I remember the day I hog-tied Naomi during Spirit Week. Instead of helping her, you counted how long it would take her to untie the rope. I know you were mad because she yelled at you and Skye."

"It took Naomi over a hundred seconds to untie that knot. How embarrassing," says Starr.

"Very embarrassing. But yes, Starr's temper is way worse than mine," says Skye.

Starr frowns. "No, it's not!"

I can't help but laugh. "I'd say both of you are equally special in your own way."

The twins smile, hug, and then hold hands. It's clear how they feel about each other. That fuzzy feeling goes away as soon as Naomi pulls up in front of me.

"Make sure you put something about the twins' party in that newspaper. And I wouldn't mind if you put something in there about how close me and twins are. That would be okay."

I point my pencil at her. "You take care of your business, and I'll take care of mine!"

"I've already told everyone in the class that I'm the twins' party planner."

She walks away, and I want to tell her that she's not as close to the twins as she thinks she is. But I can't let her get to me. I've got too much at stake with this newspaper. It takes me a long time to calm down, but I do.

Throughout the day, I stop students, office

workers, our janitor, everybody, and ask them the same question. Some answers are funny, while others are awesome. Some take the question very seriously, while others don't. When I ask Connie what makes her special, I was so sure she was going to say her painting. But she doesn't.

"I'm special because I refuse to allow anyone to stop me from believing that I'm special. Once I let someone else say, 'You're not special,' and I believe them, then they're right."

It was the best answer I'd gotten all day. Because when it was time to go home, I needed to have something that would help me stay strong.

At the end of the day, Mrs. Davis made the big announcement and wrote it on the board. "I am so delighted to present the new businesses of Bluebonnet."

David—Dancing with David
Johnny—Johnny's Jungle Juice
Mary Frances—Mary, Mary Stationery
Lisa—Lisa Loves Cupcakes
Connie and Mya—The *Texas Taradiddle* newspaper
Kenyan—Cookies from Kenyan
Naomi—Naomi's Party-Planning Company
Michael—Michael's Itty-Bitty Teeny-Weenies

Susan—Susan's Homemade Potato Chips and Dips
Skye and Starr—Two Knew You! A Fortune-
  Telling Company

Everybody claps when Mrs. Davis finishes. She's clapping, too.

"The last part of our lesson on economics will take place on April first, which also happens to be Skye and Starr's birthday! I have requested the use of the school gym for this event. I want to see you in action, as a business owner. I will give you a grade for your presentation and product. We will talk more about that tomorrow. And it looks to me that most businesses have chosen to market in the *Texas Taradiddle* newspaper. That's wonderful! However, I'm supposed to have proof of your marketing by tomorrow. Connie and Mya, when will the first edition be out?"

I don't need to look around the room to know everybody's looking at me. My mood immediately changes from "oh yeah!" to "oh no." Yesterday, when I was thinking about this, it seemed like the perfect idea. And today when I told everybody about it in the Cave, I didn't think creating a little newspaper overnight would be that big a deal. But when Connie says, "A copy of the *Texas Taradiddle* will be ready for you tomorrow morning," all of a sudden reality hits me like a slap in the face. I type with two fingers. I have no idea how to make a newspaper. I'm in a heap of trouble because the first edition of our newspaper is due tomorrow!

The applause is so loud that it hurts my ears. Words like "hurry," "urgent," "rush," "spell check," "deadline," "now," and "faster" circle my mind like an ambush. What have we done?

Good gravy in the navy. I don't feel so good.

I put my head down on my desk, because promising this newspaper by tomorrow means Connie and I may have already told the biggest taradiddle ever.

## Chapter Eleven

As soon as that bell sounds, I'm up and moving. My legs are trying to keep pace with my brain. Things are going so fast, in and out of my head, that I can't focus. As I come out of the Cave, Mrs. Davis is waiting on me.

"Mya, are you feeling better?"

"Yes, ma'am, I think so."

She bends over so that we're face-to-face. "Listen, I meant it when I said that you can talk to me about anything. I believe in communication."

"Yes, ma'am."

"Okay, see you tomorrow. I'm looking forward to

seeing the *Texas Taradiddle*!"

I dart out of my classroom, and soon I'm on the sidewalk heading home. As I *ka-clunk* toward the house, my mind shows me all kinds of things to write about in my newspaper. There's the Blue-bonnet birthday party, and the twins' party. I could write about spring, and what it feels like to be a middle child. Could I really write about that?

No. This newspaper is for good news only.

I hear Connie's boots beating the concrete behind me.

"Slow down, Mya," she says.

I do, and soon we're walking side by side as she talks to me.

"We've got a lot to do before tomorrow. We won't have time to talk to neighbors and other store own-ers today, but we can do that for our next newspaper. Have you told your parents yet? Where are we going to get our supplies?"

I shake my head. "No, I haven't told them yet, but it can't be that much to—"

Nugget and Fish catch up with us. "Why are you two walking so fast?"

"Mya and I are starting a newspaper, and we have to have the first edition ready tomorrow morning for Mrs. Davis. Just about everybody in our class is advertising in our paper to take care of the marketing part of the assignment. We're totally stressed."

"Who's putting this newspaper together?" asks Nugget.

I don't know what I was thinking, but I blurt. "Can you believe that Naomi Jackson! She's going around saying that she's been friends with the twins forever. That is such a double-Dutch lie. I've been friends with the twins longer than she has. And on top of that, she's telling everybody what to wear to the twins' birthday party!"

Nugget's voice gets loud. "Psh! Who cares what Phony Naomi thinks!"

"Nobody!" says Fish.

Nugget continues. "I know you haven't forgotten all the trouble she caused during Spirit Week. I haven't."

Fish warns me, "Stay away from her, Mya. She's a germ."

Connie shrugs. "Most of my clothes are black and white, so wearing something like that to the twins' party is no big deal to me. Can we talk about something else besides Naomi? Let's get back to the newspaper and how we're going to get it done. Nugget, you wanted to know who's putting it together?

We're going to figure it out as we go."

Fish taps me on the shoulder. "Would you like a joke to go in your newspaper? I bet that would be cool. And I can tell you what the weird calendar celebrations are for the weekend."

I grin. "That would be awesome. Can you bring those to me this afternoon?"

"Of course, Mya Papaya!"

"We need to get started as soon as possible, because when my dad gets home, he may want to use his office for something, and then we won't have a place to work."

Connie grabs one of the straps of my backpack to slow me down to a stop. "Whoa. Time out. We need to talk about supplies. You haven't told your parents about the newspaper? What about staplers and staples? How are we going to hold the newspaper together?"

"How much could a few staples cost here and—"

Connie interrupts me. "What about paper? A computer and printer ink? How are we going to pay for that?"

"I'm going to try to make a deal with my dad. Maybe he'll let us use his office supplies for twenty bucks. He lets Nugget use his office all the time."

I've never had a headache in my toes before. But

I feel pain creeping up my body. Connie puts her arm around me.

"Breathe in, breathe out. We can do this. I'll put together a start-up cost sheet for question number six. We'll know the answer to number five after you speak with your dad. I'll find the prices on the internet. That shouldn't take forever."

I'm still breathing in and out to relax. "And I'll ask my parents tonight for everything. If Dad says no, then I'll figure out another way to get supplies. The *Texas Taradiddle* is important to me, and I'll do whatever I have to do to make it happen."

"It's not just about you and me. Our classmates are depending on us to put that paper out tomorrow. They could get zeros, and it would be our fault."

"All right! I get it. Look, I can't take any more pressure, Connie. Are you coming straight to my house, or are you going home first?"

"I have to do my chores before I start on the newspaper."

"Hey, why don't you ask your parents if you can spend the night?"

"That's a good idea. I'll ask. Hopefully Mom will say yes. And I'll bring the pictures I took today with my cell phone, and some that might be good for the front page. I can download them to your dad's computer if he lets us use it. See you in a few."

As she turns off the main street to walk home, my stomach makes goink and gurgle sounds. I'm not hungry. My shoulders feel tight, and I'm not breathing normally. I can't focus on anything else at school because my mind is on how I'm going to ask my parents for supplies.

These are the same parents who have recently forgotten that they have a nine-year-old daughter. These are the parents who chose Macey and Nugget over her. And now I need them to see me, hear me, and help me.

Maybe I'll ask as a business owner instead of their daughter. Yes! Since they don't seem to see me, maybe they'll see the owner of the *Texas Taradiddle*. But I've got to make sure they're ready to hear me. I don't want to ask if they're arguing or not happy.

Mom says timing is everything. "If it's not the right time, it could definitely be the wrong time," she always says. So I wait until dinner when Mom, Dad, and Nugget are all there. Macey's asleep, so I'm careful to use my inside voice.

I put down my fork after eating every last crumb of Mom's chicken potpie. Some of that buttery crust is stuck to the roof of my mouth, but I'm sure it'll come down soon.

"That was so good. If I had a recipe for that, I'd put it in a newspaper!"

Mom smiles. "Now that's some kind of compliment. Thank you, Mya."

"You're welcome. Speaking of newspapers, I've decided to start one."

I reach underneath my chair, grab my fedora, pencil, and notepad. Dad chimes in.

"Did you say you're going to start a newspaper?"

"Yes, sir."

He chuckles. "That's the funniest thing I've heard all day! Mya, how many times have you complained about the *Bluebonnet Tribune*?"

"At least a hundred million times," I say.

He's still laughing. "So why would you want to create another one?"

Now Mom's giggling, too. "That's a good question! I would think starting a newspaper would be the last thing you'd want to do. What brought this on?"

*You did. Dad did. I had to find something to do to prove that I'm as special as Macey and Nugget.*

That's what I want to say, but I'm sure if I do, I'll get a fake-phony-full-of-baloney hug from them saying moochie-smoochie stuff like "Aw, you know we love you." Or worse, they might say, "But you're our favorite middle child."

I'm their *only* middle child! It should be against the law to have an odd number of people in a family. Somebody's always going to get left out. Maybe if we had a dog, it would make six in the family, and I''ve have something to call my own.

We don't have a dog. But I have a newspaper.

This is my moment to prove that even though my taraddidles stretch the truth sometimes, the *Texas Taraddidle* is serious. So I stand and tell them what they didn't expect to hear.

"The whole world needs a newspaper like the *Texas Taradiddle*. It is *all* good news. I may stretch a good story here and there, but it's all for fun and laughs! It's going to have advertisements, jokes, interviews, and sports stuff. What do you think?"

The dining room is creepy quiet. Nugget looks at me like I totally face-planted. Mom and Dad stare at each other before Dad clears his throat.

"This sounds very interesting, Mya, but where are you going to get your supplies? You'll need paper, and ink, which I suppose you can get from a printer, but still, those cost money, too. And who's going to do all that typing for you?"

I type with two fingers. Connie and I will

probably be up all night.

"I would like to offer you twenty dollars for use of your office equipment. And as for typing, well, I'm not that good at—"

"I am," says Nugget, interrupting me.

My mouth droops open with words sitting on my tongue that I haven't spoken yet. My eyeballs zone in on Nugget. The first thought I have is *He's going to try to mess everything up.* But then I look at his face. I know that look, and I can't help but smile a little.

"I've got a keyboarding class, and this will help me practice. We just learned how to make newspaper columns."

Dad stares at Mom. "Honey, did you hear that? I didn't learn how to type until I was a freshman! First it was economics. Now these kids are taught how to use the computer before they get out of elementary school."

*This isn't about Nugget.*

Mom shakes her head. "I know, Darrell. It's crazy."

*Stop talking about him and listen to me, please.*

Dad wipes his hands on his napkin. "And my typing skills are still horrible. They were horrible in high school!"

"Mine, too," says Mom with a giggle.

*You're going to make me . . .*

Dad keeps going. "So, Nugget, how fast can you—"

I scream. "DAD! WOULD YOU LISTEN TO ME FOR A MINUTE!"

All talking stops. Mom and Dad frown at me. Nugget stares at his plate and shakes his head. I can't move. Good gravy in the navy.

I just ruined everything for me, Connie, and all my classmates.

## Chapter Twelve

I have never raised my voice to my parents. I'm as shocked as they are. I want to say something, but I think I scared all my words back into my brain. I can't think. I can't move. But I know my parents are not happy with me. Dad tilts his head as he stares at me, as if he's trying to figure something out.

"Why are you screaming, Mya? That was very disrespectful. There's no reason for you to use that tone of voice, especially when you're talking to your parents," says Dad.

I stare at the floor and try not to cry, because I know he's right, and I already wish I could take it all back, but I can't. "I'm so, so sorry for hollering. I didn't mean to disrespect you, but I've got a school project due tomorrow, and I need to borrow paper, your computer, your printer, the stapler, and some staples."

Dad folds his arms over his chest. "Uh-huh. I see. The computer isn't a problem. Most newspapers have color in them. Printing in color is going to be expensive, but I'll cut you a deal on that. Staples are cheap. But how much paper are you talking about?"

"A lot."

"What does 'a lot' mean?" asks Mom.

Nugget tries to help me out. "After listening to everything she plans to put in it, I'm thinking she's going to need at least two, maybe three reams for her first print."

Silence again.

Dad stares at the ceiling like there's an answer up there. That's never good, because usually he's adding up the cost of something. Mom tilts her head and tucks her bottom lip inside her mouth. Another bad sign.

"Mya, are you working on this newspaper alone?" asks Dad.

"No, sir. Connie and I are partners."

"Does she have money, too?"

"Yes, sir. Her parents gave her the same amount that you gave to me."

Dad nods. "I can spare two, maybe three reams of paper. But that's going to be it. I can't do that every week. I'm sorry, but now that Macey's here, we've got added expenses that we didn't have before. So for the computer, printer, paper, and supplies, I'm charging forty dollars. You can fork over your twenty bucks now, and then call Connie to bring hers to me. Then I'll let you use the office supplies and throw in three reams of paper."

I swallow hard realizing Dad wants Connie's money, too. But we are partners, and I guess that's fair. Mom doesn't agree.

"Darrell, don't you think that's a bit harsh?"

Dad shakes his head. "This is about business, Monica. Mya's learning about economics, and I'm helping her."

"Fine," I say. "I'll call Connie and have her bring you the money when she comes over."

"And maybe this isn't something that you'll want to continue after the first week—who knows?" says Mom. "I'm proud of you for venturing out, and I'm curious to see what an all-good-news newspaper looks like. How about you, Darrell?"

Dad nods, but I can tell he's trying not to laugh. "It's all good."

Mom repeats him, like they've all of a sudden turned into Skye and Starr. "It's definitely all good."

Dad covers his mouth. Mom doesn't even try to hide her giggles.

I don't see anything funny as I had over the twenty bucks Dad gave me a few weeks ago for my economics lessons.

Mom gets serious. "We weren't laughing at you. The whole situation struck your dad and me as funny. That's all. Anyway, when do you plan for the first edition to come out?"

"Tomorrow."

Dad drops his napkin on his empty plate, stands, and heads toward the kitchen. "Three packs of paper, Mya—that's it. I can't afford to give those away. Do you understand?"

"Yes, sir. And thank you."

"You're welcome," says Mom. "Now I've got to finish Macey's Bluebonnet outfit."

I head to my room. Nugget catches up with me.

"Look, I don't think you'll need three reams for your first edition. I was just trying to get you some extra paper. One ream usually has five hundred sheets in it. That may sound like a lot, but it's not, especially when you're handing out free copies. All right. Meet me in Dad's office in thirty minutes. I'm going to call Fish before it gets too late. Maybe Connie will be here by then."

"Okay."

I grin and gently push Nugget on the shoulder. He gives me a little shove back before shuffling off to his room.

## Chapter Thirteen

I rush into Dad's office with a pencil behind my ear and at least six pieces of paper in my hand. I've made a bunch of phone calls for my front-page article, and my notes are all over these pages. Connie, Fish, and Nugget stare at me as I close the door and immediately begin to pace.

"I only have forty-five minutes before it gets dark and I have to be home," says Fish.

"Me, too," says Connie. "I gave your dad the twenty bucks. Mom said it's a school night and I can't sleep over."

"Don't worry, I'll walk you home, Connie," says Fish.

"Perfect. Okay, Mya, calm down, you're making me nervous," says Connie.

"I'll calm down when the newspaper's ready," I say.

Nugget's typing. "I've been ready to input the advertisements and articles, but you weren't here. What's the deal, Mya?"

"I had articles to write! Connie, did you bring any pictures about spring?"

"I sure did. And I did the start-up cost sheet for us. Here, take a look. Got some of the figures from the internet. Others from my parents."

| START-UP COSTS FOR THE *TEXAS TARADIDDLE* | |
| --- | --- |
| 1. RENT | $1,200 PER MONTH |
| 2. UTILITIES | $200 PER MONTH |
| 3. EQUIPMENT | $10,000 |
| 4. SUPPLIES | $500 PER MONTH |
| 5. BUSINESS CARDS | $100 |
| 6. SALARIES | $6,000 PER MONTH (FOUR PEOPLE) |
| 7. FOOD AND SNACKS | $100 PER MONTH |
| TOTAL FOR START-UP $18,100 | |

"Holy moly! Excellent job, Connie!" I say.

"With the cost of a computer, a printer, paper, staplers, staples, pens, pencils, a camera, a hand-held recorder for interviews, and a salary to Nugget and Fish—who we have to pay because they technically are our employees—and money for ourselves, our start-up cost is eighteen thousand one hundred dollars. We had twenty thousand. No loans for the *Texas Taradiddle*."

I give my newspaper partner a hug. "We make a great team."

She grins. "I know. We've been a great team since Spirit Week."

"Yes, we have," I say. I point at Fish. "You got that joke ready?"

"Sure do."

"And it's funny, right?"

"Sure is."

I clap my hands. "Okay, people, we've got a paper to put together. I've got everything for the front page right here."

"I'll download the pictures," says Connie, sitting at the computer.

I pat her on the shoulder. "Good. As soon as you're finished, I'll give Nugget the articles to type."

"Aren't newspapers supposed to be in columns?"

"Don't worry, I got that," says Nugget.

I tap my pencil on the top of my hat. "Is there something important that we're forgetting? We have a front-page article, advertisements, a tarradiddle, and a joke. Everybody look over your articles and make sure there are no spelling errors. This newspaper must be perfect."

Nugget interrupts me. "I've got spell check on the computer, so—"

I cut him off. "Spell check might not know the difference between there and their, or our, are, hour. Look, Connie and I call the shots, not you, okay? And I say everybody needs to check their spelling." I look around the room. "Any questions on that?"

It feels like all the good air left the room. And it's my fault. Did I just say those awful things to Nugget and Fish? What's wrong with me? I take a deep breath, let it out, and apologize.

"My bad. I'm having a rough day, guys. I don't know what's happening to me. Thanks for helping Connie and me make the *Texas Taradiddle* a newspaper. It's going to be awesome."

"Boo-yang awesome," says Fish.

"Incredible," says Connie.

I grin at them. "Let's work together and get this done, okay? After Connie finishes downloading those pictures, I'll give Nugget everything for the front-page articles, followed by advertisements—that's me again. Then Fish's weird calendar and jokes, and I'm going to end the newspaper with a Texas taradiddle."

The office door opens. "Keep the noise down," says Dad.

"Yes, sir, sorry," I say in a whisper.

I turn right back to my brother. "That picture's sideways. Rotate it again, Nugget. Oh, and look right there. You forgot to capitalize the first word in that sentence. What about that paragraph? Don't you think that needs to be moved to the next page because it looks stuffy and all crowded? And . . ."

He's breathing hard, through his nose, and it's very loud. I put my hand on his shoulder.

"My bad, again. I know you'll fix those things. I'm a little nervous, that's all. I wish I had my lassoing rope with me. That would calm me down."

"If you did, I'd tie you up with it and put you in a corner with a piece of tape over your mouth until I finished! Go away," he says.

I've never been hog-tied before. I've done it to one other person, and I got sent to in-school detention for it.

I pace from one end of the office to the other. I

can feel my friends eyeballing me as they stand in line to give Nugget the work they've done for the paper. After Fish and Connie give their input to Nugget, we all wait for him to put it in order on the computer.

"All right, I'm printing the first copy. Oh no. Something's wrong with the margins."

"Give it to me," I say. "It's only on the page with Fish's stuff and the advertisements. You've got to fix that, Nugget."

Silence. I look up and everyone's staring at me.

"What? Did I say something wrong? I wasn't trying to be ugly. I just want this newspaper to be perfect, that's all."

"It's going to be fine, but why are you so determined that it has to be perfect? The *Tribune* isn't perfect. They make mistakes sometimes. You need to chill out," says Connie.

"Calm down, Mya Papaya. It's all good," says Fish.

Nugget touches my shoulder. "I'll fix the margins, even if it takes me all night."

I try to smile, but the edges of my mouth won't turn upward. My friends don't understand me; there's absolutely no way they would get it. In Connie's family, she's the oldest kid. Fish is an only child. There's no middle child in their families.

I'm not going to cry like a baby to my friends about it, but I will put out a perfect newspaper. I need my parents to see my skills. And then maybe they will see *me*. Most of all, I want my parents to know that their middle kid is as good as their first and last ones.

The *Texas Taradiddle* will prove it.

# Chapter Fourteen

On Friday morning, Connie, Fish, Nugget, and I meet in front of the school. I give them stacks of the *Texas Taradiddle* to hand out. Yippee-ki-yay! It's newspaper day! The *Texas Taradiddle* is finally ready for everybody to read!

We're so early at the school that we even beat Mr. Winky to the front doors! When he sees us, a huge grin spreads across his face.

"Well, well, I love to see students so anxious to learn! Yes, yes, yes, we've got what you need inside— a big dose of education! Good morning! What do you have in your hands?"

I give him a copy of my newspaper. "Take a look at this, Mr. Winky. You're getting the very first copy of the *Texas Taradiddle*! I suggest you get yourself a cup of coffee, sit down at that big desk of yours, and enjoy the best thing to hit Bluebonnet since the Burger Bar!"

He takes a look at the front page. "This is magnificent! I'm going to save it for that cup of coffee you suggested. Yes, yes, yes! It looks like we've got us a new entrepreneur!"

A frown wrinkles my face. "This paper isn't poop, Mr. Winky. And I don't think it was very nice of you to call it extra manure."

His eyes widen. "No, no, no, Mya! I said entrepreneur, not extra manure. An entrepreneur is a person who owns their own business!"

My frown turns right-side up. "Oh! Then . . . thank you!"

I join the rest of my crew and hand out copies of the *Texas Taradiddle*. Some kids stop and read it right in front of me. One first grader is sounding out each word as he reads.

"This is good! I like it. Can I keep it?"

"Of course," I say. "This one is free, but the next one will cost you a quarter."

We're almost out of newspapers, but I hold on to

a couple to give to our janitor and the ladies in the cafeteria. I've already tucked away copies for Mom, Dad, and my neighbors. On my way to the Cave, Connie's with me as I slide one onto Mrs. Davis's desk.

"Hot off the press, just for you," I say.

"And here's our start-up cost sheet," says Connie.

Mrs. Davis picks up the start-up sheet first. "Well, I guess you two won't be needing a loan from me. But I'll need the eighteen thousand one hundred dollars from you today. Make sure you bring me that Monopoly money."

Then she looks at our paper and suddenly puts her hand over her mouth, like she's in shock or something as she reads. "This is amazing."

# THE TEXAS TARADIDDLE

Mya Tibbs—Reporter
Connie Tate—Photographer
Homer "Fish" Leatherwood—Reporter of
    Special Days and Jokes
Nugget Tibbs—Technology Expert

#  Welcome Back, Spring!

On March 21, the first day of spring, it was beautiful outside. Birds sang welcome-back songs, while frogs burped the bass to music only they can understand. But even though we may not understand what they are singing, we can feel the change, and it makes us want to dance! Welcome back, spring, and thanks for the warmth and new life you bring!

## Baseball Is Back in Bluebonnet!

It's that time again for Little League baseball. Our fall team did very well and missed the play-offs by only one game! Tryouts will be soon, so check the baseball fields for updates. Go, Bluebonnet!

## We the People of Bluebonnet Want You to Know
### *What Makes Us Special*

Mary Frances Whitaker, Fourth Grader—I have my grandma's sky-blue eyes. No one else in my family has them but me.

**Homer "Fish" Leatherwood, Fifth Grader**—
I'm special because I have a lot of friends, and a best friend named Nugget. And I made the Bluebonnet Little League baseball team.

**Lisa McKinley, Fourth Grader**—I'm special because I have really bad allergies but I don't let those allergies stop me from playing with my friends or doing what I want to do.

**Mr. Marco, Marco's Grocery**—I'm special because I was born and raised right here in Bluebonnet. I opened a grocery store, and the people of Bluebonnet support me. That makes me feel very special.

**Connie Tate, Fourth Grader**—I'm special because I refuse to allow anyone to stop me from believing that I'm special. Once I let someone else say, "You're not special" and I believe them, then they're right.

**Mr. Winky, Principal of Young Elementary School**—I am very special because I am the principal of an amazing school full of wonderful teachers and students. And I have a family at home who hugs me as soon as I walk in the door! Yes, yes, yes!

**Kenyan Tayler, Fourth Grader**—I'm special because there's absolutely nothing that I can't do if I put my mind to it.

**Britany Evans, Third Grader**—I'm special because I can read books with big words in them.

**Skye Falling, Fourth Grader**—I'm special because I have an identical twin sister. Since I'm older by a few minutes, I feel a special responsibility to take care of her.

**Starr Falling, Fourth Grader**—I'm special because I have a twin sister who looks exactly like me. She's the oldest, but I have a special desire to always take care of her.

**John Kinchlow, First Grader**—I'm special because yesterday I got a smiley face for good behavior on my take-home folder.

**Daisy Jones, Second Grader**—I'm special because I ate all my spinach last night, and Mom gave me a big hug and an extra scoop of ice cream.

**Mrs. Davis, Fourth-Grade Teacher**—I'm special because every day I get to spend a whole day with a wonderful group of students.

**Micah "Nugget" Tibbs, Fifth Grader**—I'm special because I'm good at science and so is my dad. And I have a really cool family, and a best friend named Fish.

**Mr. Sutton, Our School Janitor**—I'm special because I've witnessed this town grow to what it is today. I love seeing all the different cultures and religions. I moved to Bluebonnet forty years ago, and I can't think of any place else where I'd rather live, because the people in this town are like family. Happy birthday, Bluebonnet.

Add Your Name _____

I am special because _____

# Here's a Little Taradiddle

A hundred years ago, from as far as you could see, this land was dry as a cottonmouth rattler. Only the wind made conversation as it whistled around the hills. Settlers came and went, believing this land would never make a good place to start a home. After all, it was in the middle, in between Dallas and Fort Worth. But lo and behold, a little girl passing through with her family spotted a small field of bluebonnets so beautiful that she sat down in the middle of those flowers and refused to leave. Her family decided to spend the night, and that family never left. Soon others came, and before long, the town of Bluebonnet was born! Yee-haw!

**ATTENTION!** The second *Texas Taradiddle* newspaper will be ready next week. If you would like a copy, it will cost you twenty-five cents. Please have correct change.

## This Week's Fun Days

**Sunday:** One-Cent Day
**Monday:** Ferret Day
**Tuesday:** Find-a-Rainbow Day

**Wednesday:** Librarian Day

**Thursday:** Burrito Day

**Friday:** Student Athlete Day

**Saturday:** No Housework Day

# Advertisements

# Joke of the Week

**Question:** Why did the banana go to the doctor?

**Answer:** Because he wasn't peeling very well!

---

"Thank you, Mrs. Davis. The next newspaper will be out on Tuesday or Wednesday of next week. It will be even better!"

She gives us a hug. "Girls, this one is really good. I'm very impressed."

I've got a cowgirl strut working as I head to the Cave. There's a rhythm in my *ka-clunk* that thumps like an editor-in-chief as I head to my cabinet. I'm not sure what Connie's doing, but I bet her walk is different, too! Just as my stride gets good, I step inside the Cave. Immediately, my boots stop *ka-clunk*ing. I whisper loud enough for my own ears to hear.

"Holy moly . . ."

# Chapter Fifteen

Inside the Cave, on benches, on the floor, some sitting inside their cabinets, in total silence, are Lisa, Kenyan, David, Mary Frances, all of my classmates, reading the *Texas Taradiddle*. The twins mosey over to Connie and me, and I'm feeling like the yippee is back in my ki-yay! Lisa is the first to show us love.

"This is great! There's nothing but good news in this. It's the good-news newspaper! And I really like the taradiddle. When does the next one come out?"

"I'm not sure yet, but soon," I say.

"What was your start-up cost?" asks Kenyan.

"A little more than eighteen thousand," says Connie.

"Smart job, putting your money together," says Mary Frances.

David nods our way. "Connie, you did the photos? All of them?"

"Yep," she says with a smile.

David shakes his head. "I didn't know you had drawing *and* camera skills. That's sick."

Connie's cheeks turn rosy. "Thanks," she says.

"You're really going to charge a quarter for your newspaper?" asks Mary Frances.

I nod. "We've got to pay for the paper we used. And we need to buy our own if we want to keep the *Taradiddle* in business."

Kenyan nods. "It's worth it, Mya. I'll pay a quarter."

"Me, too," says David.

My jaw hurts from all the smiling I'm doing. But I don't care. It's a good pain.

During recess, the twins walk as fast as they can toward me with Naomi. I hear them talking, and they sound very excited.

"Don't forget to tell Connie and Mya about the cake," says Skye.

"Tell them about the cake, Naomi," says Starr.

Naomi stares at the white clouds and moves her hands around in the air as if she's creating the cake right then and there. "Black icing with white stars on it, you know, like stars in the sky! Get it?"

"Our mom isn't making our cake. We're happy because she doesn't use sugar," says Skye.

"Sugarless cakes are not good. We're happy she's not making our cake," says Starr.

"I'm going to order their cake from that new bakery in town," says Naomi.

"It's made with real sugar, and real butter," says Starr.

"We're going to eat cake and drink sugary drinks until we're super hyper," says Skye.

"Super hyper," says Starr with a giggle.

Connie giggles. "I'll be here getting hyper with you."

"Me, too," I say.

"And it's all because Naomi is planning the most awesome birthday party for us! Thank you, Naomi," says Skye.

"It's going to be awesome," says Starr.

"I mean, how long have we been friends?" asks Naomi.

"A long time," says Skye.

"A very long time," says Starr.

The twins make a big deal over Naomi like she's their best friend on the planet. But I know Naomi can be a dirty rotten person who could turn on the twins in a second! That's what she did to me. I would never do that to Starr and Skye.

I'm going to do something to remind the twins about our friendship history. It's one thing to be a middle child at home, but I refuse to be a middle friend. I can't believe it! First, Mom and Dad forgot about me, and now the twins! Am I that easy to forget? The twins are two of my most favorite people in the whole world, and I thought I was one of theirs, too. I'm deep in thought about that when the whistle blows to end recess.

The twins walk off with Naomi, almost skipping with happiness. I glance over at Connie. She puts her hand on my shoulder as we walk to get in line.

"It's no big deal, Mya. But I think I understand why you're worried. Naomi has let both of us down, and we don't want her to do the same thing to the twins."

"Yeah, that's part of it," I say. "But not all of it."

She stops me. "The answer is no. I know what you're thinking. The twins would tell Naomi to her face that you're their closest friend. But don't make them do that until Naomi gets them their cake."

I laugh. "Good point!"

We laugh and skip all the way to our line. Connie's in front of me as we walk single file back to class. She's so tall that I can't see around her, but I'm so glad she's my best friend. She even knows what I'm thinking, and how to make me feel better.

In class, we've got our history books open, and I'm staring at a bunch of soldiers fighting each other on horseback. Poor horses. I don't want to read about this. I slowly turn to look over my left shoulder. How did the twins know I was going to be looking at them? They both grin and wave. I can't help but grin at them before turning back around.

The more I think about that tiara-wearing turkey, Naomi Jackson, the madder I get. She was *not* the twins' first friend in Bluebonnet! I was!

I've known Skye and Starr since they suddenly appeared in my classroom back in first grade. It was like magic! I remember it like it was yesterday. Our first-grade teacher, Mrs. Jones, was in the middle of telling our class the difference between a long E sound and a short E sound when she stopped talking and looked toward the door. The rest of the class looked, too. No one had heard Skye or Starr come in. They were just standing there, holding hands.

Mrs. Jones spoke to them. "Hello. Can I help you?"

"We're here to learn."

And they sat down, one right behind the other in the second row, toward the back. Everybody stared as Mrs. Jones asked them if they had any paperwork. They answered together.

"No. Please call the office."

Not even a minute later, the office helper brought papers to Mrs. Jones about the two new girls at the school, and that they would soon be in her class.

"They're already here," said Mrs. Jones.

It was the strangest thing, staring at these two blond-headed, blue-eyed, freckle-faced girls who looked exactly alike. They wore the same kind of blue dress with a white collar and white around the sleeves. They smelled the same, walked the same, and didn't seem to mind that we stared at them. They smiled at me, and I couldn't help but smile back.

At lunch, they chewed their food in rhythm before taking a drink of milk. Then they both wiped their mouths with their napkins. Good gravy in the navy. It was the weirdest thing I'd ever seen.

But I think it was out on the playground that I decided we would be friends. I had a jump rope and was looking for someone to turn the other end of the rope with Lisa, but no one wanted to because Lisa has horrible allergies and sneezes on everything. Suddenly the twins began talking behind me.

"We would like to play with the rope," they said in unison.

At first I thought, *No way.* But it was either them or Lisa, better known as Miss Sneeze-a-Lot. They didn't have a problem with Lisa's sneezing, and that made me like them. So I said okay, under one condition.

"You have to stop talking at the same time. I'll never be able to tell you apart if you keep doing that."

They smiled, and Starr spoke first.

"Okay, I'm Starr."

"And I'm Skye."

"We'll stop speaking at the same time," says Starr.

"We'll definitely stop speaking at the same time," says Skye.

Since then, we've been friends, and I'm not about to give up my first-friend status to Naomi. Mrs. Davis's voice pulls me out of my thoughts.

"Class, please close your history books. It's almost time for the bell to ring, but I have one more handout for you regarding your businesses."

Some of my classmates clap. The rest of us stare at the stack of papers she's holding, wondering what we have to do now. We each take one and pass the others back, and then listen.

"All right, students, as I mentioned yesterday, the last part of your business-owning assignment will be you, as a business owner, in action, and it will take place on Friday, April sixth, in the Cave. I will grade you on your presentation and knowledge of your product."

"What does that mean?" asks Michael.

"That means your parents or grandparents can come by the Cave and pretend to be customers. I will also ask some of the school staff to participate. You will be graded on your presentation and how well you treat your customers."

"It's going to get crowded in the Cave with all of us in there," says David.

"You'll take turns. The Cave can only hold thirty people at one time. With potential customers, that would be a violation of the fire code."

I raise my hand. "I thought we were doing our presentations in the gym?"

Mrs. Davis gives me a half smile. "Me, too. I

spoke with Mr. Winky and made a request to use the gym on April sixth, but the exterminator is coming that afternoon, and he wants everybody out of that part of the school. So he couldn't let us have that day."

It's dead-people quiet in the room. Everybody's looking around. Nobody wants to have an accidental run-in with the exterminator.

Nobody.

Naomi waves her hand like it's on fire. "Mrs. Davis, I have a huge problem! If everybody is in the Cave on April sixth giving their presentations, then I can't have the twins' party in there! The Cave will be a mess! That is not fair. Can't you change the presentation day to the following Friday?"

Mrs. Davis shakes her head.

"I'm sorry, Naomi. I can't change the date because April sixth is the last day for this grading period, so I'm left with no other choice." All the good air leaves the room. I hear sniffles, like someone's crying. I'm sure it's Skye, but I can't look because I'll start crying, too.

I've got to do something. I can't let this happen to the twins. They're fired up about their party, and so is everybody else.

My thoughts drift out of the classroom, down the hall, and into Mr. Winky's office. What I'm about to ask for could be coyote crazy . . . but if I get it, everybody in my class, including Mrs. Davis, will thank me!

# Chapter Sixteen

As soon as the bell rings, I rush to my cabinet and wait for Connie. She's not walking fast enough for me, so I give her the "come here" signal with my hand.

"I'm not walking home with Nugget today. Would you please tell him? I've got business to handle."

"Don't get yourself in trouble, Mya," says Connie.

"Oh no, nothing like that. I've got an idea, and I'm going to follow through with it, that's all. Will you tell Nugget I needed to stay after school and talk with Mrs. Davis?"

"Of course. Are we still on for tomorrow?"

"Yes. I'll be ready around nine."

She hugs me, and I wait for everybody to leave before *ka-clunk*ing down the hall to our principal's office. He's not in there, and I know why. He's always somewhere around the building when the school bell rings. He helps the teachers, and even helps the younger students get on their buses, or takes them to their parents waiting in the car-ride lane.

I sit for what feels like two days, waiting for Mr. Winky to come back. Finally he appears.

"Well, well, look who I've got here! A cowgirl in my office wearing a fedora! What's the scoop? And by the way, I'm so impressed with the *Texas Taradiddle*! Yes, yes, yes!"

"Thank you, Mr. Winky. Can I speak with you in your office for a moment?"

He stretches out his arm toward his office door. "Lead the way."

The last time I was in Mr. Winky's office, I was in trouble, so I don't plan on staying long, in case he forgot to punish me for something. I sit in a chair and say what's on my mind.

"Mr. Winky, you know Bluebonnet's one hundredth birthday is coming up."

"Of course I do! The whole town is excited, and ready to celebrate in two weeks at the park!"

"That's exactly what I wanted to talk with you about, Mr. Winky. See, the fourth graders have been working on future businesses for our town. We've got some humdingers, too! We're all very proud of Bluebonnet."

"That is wonderful to hear, Mya. But I don't understand what this has to do with me."

"Next Friday, April sixth, our class would like to have permission to display the future of Bluebonnet right here in Young Elementary School's gym. Picture it, Mr. Winky. The first, second, and third graders will begin to understand what it means to take pride in their town. The fifth graders may decide that they need to do something, too! But right now, the fourth graders want to lead the way, and we need your help. I just need forty-five minutes! From three o'clock to three forty-five would be awesome. And then the program would be over."

"I've already had a conversation with Mrs. Davis about this, and I told her I would not allow students to stay after school on the day the exterminator is scheduled."

Good gravy in the navy. My heart stops beating for five whole seconds. There's got to be a way we can avoid the pest-control guy and still have that day.

"What time is he coming?"

"Five o'clock."

There are lots of rumors about the school's exterminator. I heard he wears that white uniform with that big white hat covering his head and face because the chemicals he uses cause a curse. The only reason the exterminator didn't die from the curse is because before he was an exterminator, he was a doctor, and he gave himself a shot of "reverse-the-curse" serum. But it still cost him his skin.

My classmates might chase me out of town for what I'm trying to do. I think back to what Mom said about timing. It's everything. And if we can finish our presentations quickly, then we won't even see the exterminator, and he definitely won't see us. I've got goose bumps. but I can't show any fear. I grin and slap my knee.

"Well, that's perfect! We'll be long gone by then. There won't be any signs of us anywhere in the school at five o'clock. I can guarantee you that! Please, Mr. Winky. This is very important to us."

He scratches his head and squints as if the sun is in his eyes. "Who is this program for, Mya? I'm trying to remember my converseation with Mrs. Davis."

I look at Mr. Winky's face for a clue of what he

wants me to say. I don't see anything that helps me. So I throw the question back at him!

"Who do *you* think this program should be for, Mr. Winky?"

He nods as if I've said something intelligent. I wish I could remember some of those big words I used on Nugget. They might have come in handy today. And then it hits me. I stand tall and say the words that I know Mr. Winky could never resist.

"Mr. Winky, our class is the future of this town. We're trying to show how much we care about it, and that we want to stay. Won't you help us?"

His shoulders straighten as his eyes widen and sparkle like I just sang the national anthem. "Yes, yes, yes! You are the future of Bluebonnet, and I'm so proud to be your principal! Let's see—as long as you're finished long before the exterminator comes, we might be able to do this. I think we should keep this a private production. My thoughts are that we do the presentation for the students, family members, and teachers. That way, it won't get too big."

"That's a good plan, Mr. Winky. Okay, then I'll start putting together the best rootin' tootin' good-news newspaper you've ever seen!"

"That sounds magnificent, Mya! You say you only need forty-five minutes? Does that include cleanup? Your class will have to clean up after their presentations."

"Oh, absolutely, Mr. Winky."

My heart beats with excitement at the thought that he may say yes. I want to say something else, but I'm scared it may be the wrong thing. So I keep my lips closed.

Mr. Winky rubs his chin. "I don't know, Mya. My gut says I should say no. The exterminator comes only twice a year to our school. If I miss the extermination day for any reason, then I have to wait months for another one. And I've seen a few spiders and ants in the library windowsills."

"Don't listen to your gut. Listen to me. We've worked so hard on this project. Forty-five minutes in the gym. That's all we need."

Mr. Winky leans back in his chair and scratches his head. "I guess that would leave enough time for everybody to be out of the gym before the exterminator comes."

"And we'll clean up our mess. I'll be in charge of that. We're doing this for a grade, too. Mrs. Davis plans to watch us as we talk about our future businesses to the good citizens of Bluebonnet. Can you help us out, Mr. Winky? Please?"

"You promise to be finished in the gym by three forty-five?"

"Yes, sir."

"And I won't hear any nonsense like 'We need more time'?"

"No, sir."

He sits behind his desk and stares at his calendar, and he looks at me and then at his calendar again. Finally he closes that date book and slams it on the table.

"I say let's do it! I'll get the paperwork done and get it on the school calendar. But remember, Mya, the invitations should be only for teachers, students, and their families. How do you plan to let the teachers and students know?"

"I'm going to advertise it in the *Texas Taradiddle*," I say.

"Now that's a great idea! Okay, you have my permission."

Both of my arms lift to the ceiling. "Woo-hoo! Thank you, Mr. Winky. You won't be disappointed. It's going to be a great day for Young Elementary School, showing our spirit."

I skedaddle out of his office and head home. I'm sure Connie's already home, but it doesn't matter.

I'm so excited that I got something done that Mrs. Davis didn't think could happen!

But best of all, I'll get to show the twins that I'm the ultimate friend. I'm doing this for everybody, including Mrs. Davis. But it will be extra special for the twins, because they'll get their grade for their presentation and all that, and then have their birthday party!

Mr. Winky said we had to be out of the gym by three forty-five. He didn't say we had to be out of the school! So if the exterminator comes at five, that gives us over an hour to have fun! Everybody is going to be so happy with me.

Maybe this is the beginning of everything going right instead of going wrong. I've heard people say that it always gets worse before it gets better. Well, today was the worst, so maybe that saying is true!

## Chapter Seventeen

After school, I skip home. I've got Mom's and Dad's copies of my newspaper in my backpack, in case they want to frame them. I'm so excited, thinking about all the wonderful things that will happen for me today at home.

Maybe Dad will give me a new nickname. He calls Macey baby girl. I think he should start calling me his baby doll or little girl! Yeah!

The house is quiet when I walk inside. That's how it's been for a while now, so we don't think anything of it. I tiptoe into the kitchen to see Mom. She's not there. I check her room. Nope.

In the nursery, I find her in the rocking chair asleep, with Macey in her arms. She must've had a rough day. I take off my boots and quietly walk over to Mom and Macey. They're both in a deep sleep. I gently take Macey out of Mom's arms and put her in her crib. As soon as I lay her down, she begins to whimper, and then that turns into a full-blown cry.

"*Waaaaah! Waaaaaaaaah!*"

Mom rushes over to the crib. "Why did you move her? She was finally asleep."

I can't find my words. Mom's face has a lot of mad in it, and I'm not sure what I did wrong. "You were both sleeping and I was trying to help you sleep better, that's all."

Mom shakes her head. "She's teething, and I've tried everything, but all she's done today is cry. I finally get her to sleep, and you move her."

"I'm sorry, Mom."

Her hair is a mess. She looks like she hasn't slept in days. And she sounds so miserable.

"No, I'm not blaming you, Mya. It's not your fault. I'm just so tired. And somehow I made Macey's little Bluebonnet outfit she's supposed to wear to the birthday bash too small. I have to start over."

"If you show me what to do, I can stay up with Macey and hold her while she's teething. You can go finish your nap or go work on Macey's outfit."

"No, but thanks. Your dad will be home soon. I called him earlier today, and he said he would shut down around four o'clock instead of six. He should be walking in the door any minute. Where's your brother?"

I shrug. "Probably upstairs in his room. But Mom, I know you're tired and I'm really sorry that Macey's teething, but I've got something to show you."

As I rush to the living room to get my backpack, I hear Mom holler. "Not right now, Mya. There's no way I can look at anything, because I'm so tired I can barely see. But if you leave it on the coffee table in front of the sofa, I promise to take a look."

It's not just looking at my newspaper. I need to *tell* her about it. I want her to know that she was the one who gave me the idea, and I was able to make it happen. She needs to know that I can do lots of things, like her. I need to see Mom's and Dad's faces when they read my newspaper and realize that I created it. How long could we sit and talk about my newspaper? Probably a long time!

Most of all, I need her to know I'm special, too.

"Did you hear me, Mya?"

Macey's still crying. That's what I hear. "Yes,

ma'am. I'll put it on the coffee table."

I take both copies of my newspaper out of my backpack and put them in the center of the coffee table in the living room. They have the whole weekend to look at them. There's no way Mom or Dad can miss them. They come into the living room just about every night after dinner. I can wait that long to hear from them!

Dad's home early and makes soup for dinner. Macey's asleep, and so is Mom. At the table, Dad looks so tired that I think his face is going to drop into his bowl of soup. I shuffle over and nudge him.

"Dad!"

His head snaps back, and his eyes widen. "Yeah, yes, I'm here. What happened?"

Nugget giggles, but I don't think it's funny at all. "Dad, you're falling asleep."

"I'm sorry. It's been a long day. I need some sleep, and then I can take shifts with your Mom to take care of Macey. She's teething."

"I know. But Dad, I left something on the coffee table for you and Mom to look at. It's something I did, and I really, really need for you to look at it, okay?"

He nods. "I'm going to lie down for about an hour, and then I'll check it out, okay?"

I grin. "Okay, thanks, Dad."

He gets up, goes to his room, and closes the door. Nugget and I sit alone at the table.

"You think he's going to wake up and look at my newspaper?"

Nugget shrugs. "I've never seen him look that tired. But if Mom and Dad are taking shifts to care for Macey, then it's possible that he'll see it. Or Mom might see it."

Nugget and I clean off the table together. I go to my room, lasso a few farm animals, do my homework, listen to some country and western music, and then go to bed.

# Chapter Eighteen

Early Saturday morning, I race downstairs to get all of my "Good job, Mya!" and "Your newspaper is amazing, just like you!" compliments from Mom and Dad. A quick glance at the table in the living room lets me know that's not going to happen. The copies of the *Texas Taradiddle* are in the same place I left them.

The exact same place.

I take the last two steps very slowly, trying to think of a reason why they wouldn't have looked at it. Maybe they forgot. Maybe they were tired. Maybe they're going to look at it today! Yeah, that's what's going to happen. Dad has to work, but he'll be home later, and the *Taradiddle* will be the perfect newspaper for him to read while he's relaxing.

I make a bacon and egg sandwich out of the breakfast Mom made, and head to the door with a new dose of hope. Connie's waiting for me on the porch.

"Hi. You ready?" she asks. "What'd your parents say about the newspaper? Mine went ape crazy! They made such a big deal out of it!"

"Yep, but we've got a lot of stuff to talk about."

Connie smiles. "I know, so let's get started. I'm excited!"

We talk as we walk through our neighborhood about what we'd like to have in the next newspaper and what it's going to be like in the gymnasium next Friday.

"We need lots of pictures," says Connie.

"Speaking of pictures, have you started yours yet? You know, the one you're doing for the Bluebonnet party in the park? You haven't said two words about it in almost a week. Are you going to do it or back out?"

"I haven't started yet, and I'm getting really nervous about it. Something's got to happen to make me want to paint it. I'm still waiting on whatever that is. Can we not talk about it?"

I put my hand on her shoulder. "Sure. Let's talk about articles for the paper. It has to be good stuff, not bad news. And the pictures you take with the camera have to go with the articles."

Across the street, Mrs. Hampton is sweeping her garage. She waves. "Hello, Mya. Hi, Connie."

At first, I wave back, but then I realize I may be missing out on a news opportunity. I holler from across the street.

"Hey, Mrs. Hampton. We're starting a newspaper. Do you have anything you would like to advertise in our paper? It will only cost you five dollars."

As soon as she nods, Connie and I dash over to her house. Mrs. Hampton poses as Connie snaps a picture of her sweeping. I flip my notepad to a clean page and grab the pencil sitting behind my ear.

"Okay, what's the scoop?"

I cut my eyes to Connie and grin. Asking for "the scoop" makes me feel like a real news reporter. Connie grins back and takes another picture of Mrs. Hampton.

"Next Saturday, I'm having a big garage sale," says Mrs. Hampton. "I'll have lots of dishes, electronic equipment, clothes, books, shoes, fishing poles, all kinds of things for sale."

I'm writing like crazy but still ask, "Are you selling your stuff cheap?"

She shrugs. "No reasonable offer will be turned down! And if a customer buys something, I may give them something else for free!"

Connie takes a picture of Mrs. Hampton's Honda Accord. "You might give away your car for free?"

I stop writing. "Jambalaya! You're giving away a car? That's big-time news!"

"Oh no, no, no! Don't write that in your newspaper, Mya. I need my car. But there will be other things that will be free for paying customers."

We shake hands. "I'll make sure this article about your garage sale gets in our newspaper. It's called the *Texas Taradiddle*, and the next copy comes out on Tuesday."

"Thank you, Mya. Thanks, Connie. See you later."

We head down the sidewalk and Connie points at a sign. "Let's go over to the new bakery. Maybe we'll get a free cookie."

I'm all for free cookies, so we skedaddle across the street to the Cake Bake.

*Cling-aling-aling!*

It sounds more like a bicycle bell than a bell that goes over a door, but it seems to work fine. Just as we walk in, Naomi scoots her chair away from a table near the window.

"What are you two doing here?" she asks.

"We're getting advertisements for the *Texas Taradiddle*," I say.

Connie's quiet, but she's staring at Naomi with that old Mean Connie Tate face she used to have when I first met her.

A lady comes out from the back with papers in her hand. "Okay, Miss Jackson. Your cake order will be ready on the first, and here's your copy of the paperwork. Thank you."

"You're welcome," says Naomi. She turns to Connie and me.

"Ordering the twins' cake. I'm handling my business, too. See you later."

Naomi opens the door.

*Cling-aling-aling.*

Once she's gone, Connie's face goes back to normal. The lady in the store greets us.

"Good afternoon. Can I help you?"

I'm about to talk about the newspaper, but Connie yells out, "You got any free cookies?"

The lady grins as she walks toward the back. "You're in luck today. What's your name?"

"Connie."

I use my outside voice so she can hear me in the back. "And I'm Mya Tibbs, with the *Texas Tara-diddle*."

The lady comes out with two big chocolate chip cookies and two napkins. I almost forgot what I was talking about when she hands me mine. She extends her hand. "It's nice to meet you, Connie and Mya. My name is Martha Jacobs, and I'm the owner of the Cake Bake."

We thank her, but I keep talking as Connie eats her cookie. "We're starting a newspaper and wanted to know if you'd like us to advertise about your new bakery."

Connie stops chewing, steps in front of me, and wipes the crumbs from the sides of her mouth. "Advertising isn't free. It's going to cost you five dollars per month. Our newspaper is good news only, and almost every kid at our school gets a copy. Think about that."

Connie and I take big bites of our cookies and wait for Ms. Jacobs to respond.

"I would love to advertise my new bakery in your newspaper!"

The cookie's so good that I give Ms. Jacobs my notepad and let her write her information down. When she's finished, she hands me my notepad and five dollars. I give the money to Connie.

"Good luck with your newspaper, Mya and Connie."

"Thanks, and good luck with your new bakery," I say.

"Your cookies are good," says Connie. "You have to have a good product to stay in business. And your presentation was excellent. I'd say you've got a shot at making it here."

Ms. Jacobs's face lights up with happiness. She's got a smile that stretches wider than the Mississippi River. "Thanks, Connie. I hope to be in business here a long time."

"Would you mind if I take a few pictures of your place for the *Texas Taradiddle*?"

"No, not at all."

After Connie gets her photos, we leave the bakery and head back toward my street.

"Let's go over to Mrs. Rodriguez's house. She's a really nice lady," I say.

Connie's got her camera ready, and I'm ready too with my notepad and pencil.

*Knock, knock.*

Mrs. Rodriguez opens the door and gives Connie and me a big smile. "Hola, señoritas! How are you today? Are you selling Girl Scout cookies?"

I shake my head. "We've started a newspaper called the *Texas Taradiddle*. And it's going to have nothing but good news in it. Do you have anything you'd like to advertise in our paper, Mrs. Rodriguez?"

"How much will it cost me?" she asks.

"Five dollars for a month."

"Why, yes, I do! My Chihuahua, Chica, had cinco cachorros! Come see!"

Mrs. Rodriguez hurries back into her house. I turn to Connie.

"I know cinco means five in Spanish, but what does cachorros mean?"

Connie shrugs. "I think cachorros are those really good fried cinnamon sticks with sugar on them. If Chica ate five, she's calling Larry."

"Who's Larry?"

Connie rolls her eyes and pretends she throwing up. "Laaarrrry."

I frown. "Ew. I don't want to see a barfing Chihuahua."

"She's got to be one miserable dog. And if those cachorros were still warm when she ate them . . . I don't want to see that, either," says Connie as she puts her camera away.

My family has known Mr. and Mrs. Rodriguez

since they moved here three years ago. Mom made a pie, and our whole family went over and welcomed them to Bluebonnet. They don't have any children, and I wasn't very happy about that. How could a perfectly good house, just waitin' for sleepovers and birthday parties, get sold to people with no kids?

But the day we met her, Mrs. Rodriguez was holding Chica, her Chihuahua, and that cute little dog licked my face and made me giggle. So I wasn't mad at the Rodriguezes anymore for not bringing new kids for me or Nugget to play with. They had Chica.

Mrs. Rodriguez's voice startles me out of my thoughts.

"Come see!" she says.

Connie sighs and takes my hand. "Let's get it over with."

I let Connie go first. She steps inside the house, and I'm right behind her. The living room is right as you walk through the door, like our house.

Mrs. Rodriguez points to a big box in the living room. I take a bunch of short breaths so I can hold one long one in case Chica's done something gross. Connie and I stop in front of the box. We look inside together. We let go of each other's hands.

"Puppies!" I say.

"Yes! Cachorros! Puppies!" says Mrs. Rodriguez.

Connie takes her camera out and snaps three pictures. "May I pick one up?"

"Sí! Yes!" says Mrs. Rodriguez.

Connie and I reach inside the box and pick up the cutest puppies in the history of cute puppies. Mine has brown hair with a streak of white running from the tip of its nose, in between its eyes, to the top of its head! Connie's puppy is shiny black with a white streak running from his nose to the top of his head. And his paws are white! It looks like he's wearing socks!

Suddenly the puppy I'm holding begins to cry. It sounds like Macey when she's hungry! I put the puppy back in the box, just in case I'm right.

And I was.

Chica lies on her side, and her puppies begin to drink milk from her. Connie puts her puppy back in the box so it won't miss the meal. That's when I notice that all of the puppies have a streak running from their nose to the top of their heads. Some are black with a brown streak, with brown on their chest and paws. I turn to Mrs. Rodriguez.

"We'll be sure to put your good news in our paper. How much are you selling these puppies for?"

Mrs. Rodriguez hands me five dollars. "No! I

give cachorros away! Free to good home. Must be good home, Mya," she says, shaking her finger.

I hand the money to Connie and write on my notepad. "Got it. Free to good homes. I'll put something special in my newspaper about it, and you'll have a line of people at your door wanting Chica's . . . cachorros. We have to go now. Adiós, Mrs. Rodriguez!"

Connie takes one more picture before heading toward the door. "Adiós, Mrs. Rodriguez."

"Adiós, and gracias, Mya and Connie."

As soon as we're on the sidewalk, I make a few more notes on my pad. Connie puts her hand on my shoulder. "We've got a problem, Mya. To be fair to Mrs. Rodriguez, to try to get people to come and get her puppies, we need to distribute the newspaper all over Bluebonnet."

I shrug. "Yeah, so what's . . . oh, I forgot. Mr. Winky said just to the school."

"What are we going to do?"

"It's not fair to all of the people advertising in our newspaper for us to limit who gets the paper. That's wrong."

"Mya, there's no way you can get a line of people waiting outside Mrs. Rodriguez's door for puppies, even if they are free. Not from just kids and teachers at our school."

I put my pencil behind my ear and stuff my notepad in my back pocket. "I can if I tell everyone the cachorros are bilingual. They cry in English, like regular babies . . ." I grin at Connie, and wink. "But as they get older, they'll bark in Spanish."

Connie giggles. "That's a great idea, Mya! I should have taken more pictures! How many people have bilingual puppies?"

I hold up one finger. "There's only one place in Bluebonnet to get 'em, and you'd better have a copy of our newspaper to know exactly where they are, because she's only got five. We have to tell the world! Come on, Connie! Good news is waiting, and we need to find it!"

Connie and I beat the streets of Bluebonnet all weekend. On Sunday, once we think we've got enough for the newspaper, we head home.

"I hope this second one is going to be as good as the first one," says Connie.

"That first newspaper was so good. This one will be, too."

I get home and open the door as Nugget is walking up the stairs. Mom's in the living room. Before I can say anything, she puts her finger to her mouth for me to be quiet. I glance at the coffee table. My newspapers are in the same place where I left them.

No. That can't be.

I get closer and look for signs that they've been read, like wrinkled pages or even a coffee or food stain on the front. But being this close only proves what I hoped wasn't true, and my brain reminds me of things I don't want to hear.

I'm not special. If I was, my parents would have read the *Texas Taradiddle*. But they don't see my newspaper because I don't matter. I'm not as good to them as Nugget and Macey. I'm wasting my time trying to get them to notice my skills, because no matter how hard I try, I can't make Dad stop thinking about the price of corn. I can't make Mom talk to me. I can't make them stop arguing at the table. My plan didn't work. I can't make my family happy again.

I hold the sides of my head, believing this is the only way to stop myself from caving to the floor. I clamp my teeth together, hoping I don't let out the cry that's sitting in my throat, because it will definitely wake the baby. I kick off my boots, grab the phone, and head to my room as tears flood my face.

I'm not alone. I have a really good friend, and she's my newspaper partner, too! I can't focus on what's going on at home right now. I need to work on the *Texas Taradiddle*. We're going to make it the best good-news newspaper ever created!

I'm not going to think about my family. Soon, I won't even cry about them anymore. I won't wonder what kind of faces Macey's making. I won't care if my parents don't understand what she's trying to say.

Connie and the *Texas Taradiddle* are my new family.

# Chapter Nineteen

I thought the newspaper would make me stand out instead of keeping me in the middle, but it didn't. I thought Mom and Dad would glow with pride when they saw what I did. I guess they have enough to glow about with Macey and Nugget. They don't even need me.

Mom approaches me. "How many braids this morning, Mya?"

"A ponytail is fine."

I don't want any braids. Mom doesn't even ask me why. And I don't ask her why she let a perfectly good good-news newspaper sit on the coffee table all weekend and not read it.

Why am I even writing a good-news newspaper when I feel so bad?

I walk to school with Nugget, but we don't say two words to each other. I don't know if he's got a problem with me, or if he knows I'm unhappy. Either way, I don't care, because I don't want to talk.

Mrs. Davis stops me when I enter the classroom. "That sure is a long face for a cowgirl. Are you sure you're okay?"

I don't want Mrs. Davis worrying about me. I want her to think that everything is great. She doesn't need to know what's going on at my house. So I change the subject to something I think she'd like.

"On Friday, after school, I went to Mr. Winky's office and talked to him about us using the gym for our presentations on April Fool's Day. I spoke to him as a business owner, like you would want me to, Mrs. Davis. And Mr. Winky said yes, yes, yes!"

Mrs. Davis's eyes widen. "Are you serious? What about the exterminator?"

"We have to clean up our mess and be out of the gym by three forty-five."

She stands and hugs me. "Right! This is the best news! I don't know how you convinced him to do that! He gave me a flat no when I asked him."

I lean on Mrs. Davis's desk. "I reminded him that we're the future of Bluebonnet. He loves this town, and he loves us. It was easy-peasy once I put those two things together."

Mrs. Davis shakes her head. "But . . . wait, you do realize that the twins' birthday party is on Friday, right?"

"Oh yes, ma'am. That's the beauty of the whole thing. See, the twins will get their grade from you for their presentation, and then leave from the gym and go straight to the Cave for their party. The presentations will last from three to three forty-five. And then we'll have the twins' party from three forty-five to four forty-five. Mr. Winky said the exterminator comes at five. We'll be gone by then. I didn't mention the party to Mr. Winky. He doesn't need to give us permission for that, right?"

Mrs. Davis shakes her head. "Well, it sounds to me like you've got it all worked out!"

"Thanks, Mrs. Davis, but please don't mention anything to my classmates yet. I want to tell them tomorrow, when they're reading the Special Birthday Edition of my newspaper."

She pretends she's zipping her lips. "Not a word from me."

I fake a smile and keep going. In the Cave, I feel one hundred percent different than I did on Friday when I was in here. Everybody was congratulating me, telling me how awesome I am, and making me feel amazing. I was on top of the world, skipping all the way home.

Today, I feel alone. No one knows what it feels like to be in my position. I haven't heard one person in my class say anything about the things I'm going through.

Lisa comes over to me. "Hey, Mya, are you okay?"

"I'm good," I say, nodding my head.

"You don't look so good," says Skye.

"You really don't," says Starr.

"I'm good, really," I say with another fake smile.

Connie's watching me. I can feel her eyes burning like a laser in the side of my head. Once Lisa and the twins walk away, she writes something on a piece of paper and holds it up to me.

*You want to talk?*

I shake my head, because I do want to talk but I don't want to cry, and if I start talking I know a river of tears is going to pour out of my eyes. My best friend puts her arm around me.

"I'd say let's talk at lunch, but it's cheese pizza day, and you know how much I love cheese pizza. If you decide you don't want yours, I'll eat it. Maybe I'll come out at recess today instead of painting. Then we can talk."

I toss my backpack into my cabinet and close it. "You don't have to do that."

Connie steps closer. "You're my best friend, Mya. Something's wrong, and I'm not going to stop asking you until I get to the bottom of it. That's what a good reporter does, right?"

I shrug, *ka-clunk* toward the classroom, and take a seat. For the whole morning I avoid turning around and looking at Connie, because I don't want her worrying about me.

At lunch, Connie holds true to what she said. There's no talk at our little table as I watch her kill her two pieces of cheese pizza, and mine, too. I drink my milk and chew on a few carrot sticks. That's it.

When it's time for recess, Mrs. Davis gives out all the rubber balls. She tosses one right to me, and I let it hit the asphalt and bounce toward Lisa. Mrs. Davis tilts her head, and I turn away.

I've never felt this down before. I don't know if there is anything that can help me smile again. Maybe my face is stuck this way. There's no one sitting underneath the big oak tree today, so I take a seat and grab a few blades of grass. Someone plops beside me. The noise makes me jump until I notice it's Connie.

We sit in silence for a few moments, and then she speaks. "Have you been spreading the word about the newspaper being on sale in the morning?"

I nod. "To everybody I see. Fish and Nugget have been telling people, too. I think it's going to be a big deal."

"Okay, Mya, something's wrong with you. I can tell. You want to talk about it?"

My jaw tightens. "I don't think you'd understand, Connie."

She throws a blade of grass at me. "Remember when we were Spirit Week partners, and you came looking for me in my art room because you thought something was wrong?"

"Yes, I remember."

"There was something wrong, but I didn't think you'd understand. Turns out you totally understood me, and we ended up being best friends." She takes my hand, like a good friend would. "Mya, if I don't get it, I'll tell you."

I try not to cry, but can't help it. "Okay."

I dig at the dirt around me and try to figure out

exactly what I want to say. But the more I think about it, the more I'm scared that Connie will think I'm acting like a baby.

"Come on, Mya, we don't have much time left at recess. What's wrong?"

"I'm not special."

"What?"

"There's nothing about me that stands out. And because of that, my parents don't remember to talk to me, or hug me, or ask me to help them. I hate being the middle child."

"Oh, Mya, I'm so sorry. I guess it really is true that being a middle child is tough. It's so hard to believe, because you've got the best parents in the whole world."

"Remember before Macey was born, when I thought Mom would forget about me? Well, it's worse than that. Mom and Dad love on Macey because she's so cute, and she really, really is. And they give Nugget things to do for them because he's so smart. But me, I don't have anything to give to them. I'm not cuter than Macey, and I'm not smarter than Nugget. At least when Mom was still pregnant, she tried to do things with me."

Connie agrees. "She did teach us how to make good chili. You almost won that contest."

I shake my head. "But we're not doing anything like that now. It's as if she's got a new baby, and it replaced the old one. And it's even worse with Dad. He's showing Nugget everything about the store and has no time for me."

Connie keeps picking grass with me. "Oh. It's kind of like you've become . . ."

"Something in the middle," I say.

"Like my friend Maria Escobar," says Connie. "We went to private school together before I started going to this school."

I look up, hoping Connie's about to give me some miracle advice. But she doesn't.

"Yeah, after her baby brother was born, Maria said her parents acted like she didn't exist. I don't think she did anything except stay mad all the time. She used to be so nice, but then she became mean and stayed to herself. I know she started making videos online, talking about lots of different stuff, but most of it was her going off about how terrible it is being a middle child. But the videos gave her something to do, I guess."

"Like the *Texas Taradiddle*."

Connie shrugs. "Yeah, I guess so. The newspaper is really good, Mya. Think about that, and stop worrying about stuff that will make you mad and sad.

And talk to your parents. I don't want you to be like Maria Escobar."

I stand and wipe the dirt from my pants. "I don't want to be like her, either. But I understand how she feels. Her parents forgot about her. Why should she have to tell them what they're doing wrong? Can't they see that on their own?"

Connie gives me a big hug. "I see you. And you're special to me."

Air I didn't even know I was keeping in my belly slowly leaves through my nose. I close my eyes and hug my best friend back. She really does understand me.

"Have you decided what picture you're going to paint for Bluebonnet's party?"

"Not yet, but I'm working on it. Right now, I want to talk about the newspaper. This afternoon, let's get the word out to everybody!"

It felt good to smile. "The *Texas Taradiddle* is here! Sounds like a plan!"

The smile quickly slides from my face as I think about what Mr. Winky said. "Connie, I don't think it's fair that Mr. Winky said I could only distribute our newspaper to the teachers and students and families. What about the people who advertised with us, like our neighbors and Ms. Jacobs at the

Cake Bake? That's not really fair, but I guess I have to do what he said."

Connie shrugs. "The only thing I can think of is that you put a note before the article about our presentation and say that it's only for teachers, students, and family members. That way we can still hand out the newspaper to everybody!"

"Yes! That's a perfect idea! I'm going to put that note in the newspaper about our presentation!"

I thought the second edition would be easier, but it wasn't. Nugget, Fish, Connie, and I work even harder on this edition than we did on the first one.

On Monday, after school, we set a stack of newspapers aside to take to school tomorrow morning, and then take the remaining copies to as many stores as we can. Some businesses let us leave a bunch of copies, and pay us a quarter for each of them. Some let us leave one, and give us a quarter. But we sell at least sixty copies of our newspaper around town.

Tomorrow, we release our Special Birthday Edition at school, and I can't wait to see the twins' faces!

# Chapter Twenty

Tuesday morning, Connie and I head to school forty-five minutes early. We've got so much stuff in our backpacks that it's pulling down our shoulders as we walk. Connie even remembered to bring a can for collecting money.

She leans toward me. "Are you going to tell everybody that Mr. Winky said we could use the gym?"

I nod. "Today's the perfect day, since it's talked about in the newspaper."

I can't believe Nugget and Fish keep asking for free copies of the *Texas Taradiddle*. There's no way I'm letting anyone have this issue for free.

Not even my gasconading, bumfuzzled brother.

"Come on, Mya! This isn't fair. I'm your brother, and I shouldn't have to pay. I worked hard on that paper!"

Fish is on the other side of me. "And I'm your . . . well, your really good friend. That should mean something, right? And I worked on the newspaper, too!"

Connie giggles, but I give them a straight answer without smiling.

"No special treatment for the Special Birthday Edition!"

My boots *ka-clunk* the sidewalk a little harder as I make my way to school. Up ahead there's a crowd of kids standing outside near the flagpole. A few point my way, and soon they look like a herd of cattle. I yell at the top of my lungs.

"Stampede!"

I'm about to make a new path through the grass when I see Starr and Skye leading the crowd. One of the kids behind them hollers, "I want the *Texas Taradiddle* Special Birthday Edition! I've got my quarter!"

"Me, too!" yells another kid.

Connie and I let the straps of our backpacks slide down our arms, take out our stacks of the Special Birthday Edition, and then set our can on the sidewalk. Nugget gets a quarter from his pocket. Fish takes one from his as they stand first and second in a long line. I cover the can so they can't put their money in.

"The first two copies of the *Texas Taradiddle* Special Birthday Edition go to Starr and Skye. And they are the only ones who get a free copy. Everybody else pays."

I hand a copy to Skye and one to Starr. "I hope you like it. If you don't understand what I did, I'll explain it to you later, okay?"

"I'm sure we'll love it. And this quarter is for Mr. Winky's copy," says Skye.

"We'll love it, and so will Mr. Winky," says Starr as she takes her sister's hand and skips toward the school door.

I look up to see Mr. Winky waving from the front door.

Nugget drops his quarter in the can. "I can't believe you made us pay."

The sound of his coin clinking the bottom of the can sends goose bumps all over me! I begin to yell out to everyone in line.

"Extra, extra, read all about it! The *Texas Taradiddle* Special Birthday Edition will cost you a quarter!"

Connie yells out, too. "Get your copy now, before it's too late!"

I've never seen a line this long! Not even on cheese pizza day in the cafeteria. With ten minutes to go before the bell rings, Connie and I shut everything down. The oatmeal can is heavy as I drop it into Connie's backpack. The coins clank with every step she takes. Mr. Winky's there and greets me as I walk in.

"Hello, hello, hello, little Ms. Entrepreneur. And that's 'preneur,' not manure like you thought I had said before. I hope this one is as good as your last. I'm so proud of you and Connie! Have a YES kind of day today, Mya."

"Thank you, Mr. Winky."

Mrs. Davis smiles when I step inside the classroom.

"I have my quarter. You're not sold out, are you?"

I hand her a copy. "No, ma'am. I can't believe how many copies Connie and I sold in just thirty minutes!"

Mrs. Davis hugs me. "You did a great job of marketing it yesterday. All the teachers plan on getting copies. I'm sure you'll be sold out by the end of the day. Are you going to tell your classmates about the gym?"

"Yes, ma'am."

I'm a few steps away from the Cave, and I bet all my classmates are in there waiting on me. They stood in that long line this morning to get their copies. I'm sure they're finished reading it by now. I can't wait to hear what they think. I might get a standing ovation!

I've never felt like this. Everybody in the whole school wants a copy of the Special Birthday Edition of the *Texas Taradiddle*. I'm famous, a star, a big-time newspaper editor, and on my way to making a name for myself at school.

When I step inside the Cave, all eyes are on me. Johnny steps forward with a copy of the *Texas Taradiddle* in his hand. He holds the paper up as he talks.

"We just finished reading the front page. We can't do our presentations in the gym on Friday. Isn't that the day the exterminator comes?"

I look around the room before answering. I also look for another exit besides the entrance to the Cave in case things get out of hand. I take a deep breath, and talk with all the confidence I have.

"Okay. Let me finish before you say anything. Yes, it's exterminator day, but we'll be long gone, probably doing homework or playing outside our homes by the time the exterminator gets there. I've got it all worked out. And if we follow my plan, we'll be gone a whole fifteen minutes before he even parks his pest-control truck in the school parking lot."

"You better not blow this, Mya," says Michael.

"If that exterminator gets anywhere near me—" says Lisa.

"Relax. It's going to be awesome. And I did it for everybody. I wanted all of us to get our presentations finished, and then party with the twins on the same day! How cool will that be? And this way, Naomi gets her grade for the party, too! Everybody wins!"

It's quiet again. Suddenly David steps forward and holds out his fist for me to bump.

"I think you're right, Mya. This April Fool's Day is going to be awesome. Let's do it!"

Heads begin to nod. Smiles come back. I'm getting high fives, pats on the back, fist bumps, and hugs. It feels like the best day ever. I feel needed, like someone wants me around. The exact opposite of how I feel at home.

# THE TEXAS TARADIDDLE

Mya Tibbs—Reporter
Connie Tate—Photographer

Homer "Fish" Leatherwood—Reporter of
Special Days and Jokes
Nugget Tibbs—Technology Expert

# Special Birthday Edition

*Skye and Starr Falling Will Be Ten Years Old!!!*
*Bluebonnet, Texas, Will Be One Hundred Years Old!!!*

Ten years ago, on April first, twin girls were born to the Falling family. They named those wonderful girls Skye and Starr. The Falling family moved to Bluebonnet, Texas, when Skye and Starr were in first grade. I remember very well because we quickly became friends. And we are still friends. So today I want to take this front-page space to give a shout-out to my favorite twins, Skye and Starr Falling, on their tenth birthday. Happy birthday. From Mya.

One hundred years ago, on April ninth, Bluebonnet, Texas, became a town. The men and women of Bluebonnet worked hard to make this town their own. Many family members of the first business owners and homeowners of Bluebonnet still live in this town. So I would also like to take this front-page space to give a shout-out to the best little town in Texas. Happy birthday, Bluebonnet! From Mya.

# Bluebonnet's Future Business District on Display

*THIS EVENT IS NOT OPEN TO THE PUBLIC. ONLY STUDENTS AND TEACHERS OF YOUNG ELEMENTARY, AND THEIR FAMILIES, ARE INVITED.*

**When**: Friday, April 1
**Where**: Young Elementary School Gym
**Time**: 3:00 to 3:45

In honor of the one hundredth birthday of Bluebonnet, Texas, the students of Mrs. Davis's fourth-grade class will present their new-business ideas. Here's a sample of the businesses that will be in the gym on Friday.

**Dancing with David:** Learn all the latest dance moves, and even some of the old ones!

**Lisa Loves Cupcakes:** Want a sample? Better get there early!

**Naomi's Party-Planning Company:** It's not a real party unless Naomi Jackson planned it!

**Cookies from Kenyan:** Best cookies this side of the Mississippi River!

**Mary, Mary Stationery:** Personalize your letterhead and envelopes!

**Susan's Homemade Potato Chips and Dips:** You gotta try this!

**Two Knew You! A Fortune-Telling Company:** Think you've been here before? You have!

**Johnny's Jungle Juice:** Try the Tarzan Tropical Treat!

**Michael's Itty-Bitty Teeny Weenies:** Mini hot dogs in barbecue sauce!

# WHAT'S GOING ON AT YOUNG ELEMENTARY SCHOOL?

KINDERGARTEN: I am learning about shapes, colors, and letters. Our teacher said there are four different seasons, but my dad said there are only two: summer and huntin'.

*Bubba, Kindergarten*

FIRST GRADE: I am reading and spelling and learning about regular nouns and professional nouns called pronouns for short. And we're learning about coins, but it's kind of dumb that a nickel is bigger than a dime.

*Sally, First Grade*

SECOND GRADE: I don't like all this home-work. But I do like writing stories.

*Zach, Second Grade*

THIRD GRADE: I'm too old to play with action figures, but I think Wonder Woman could beat up Batman. Third grade is kind of weird except I like learning about the solar system.

*Amanda, Third Grade*

**FOURTH GRADE:** Fourth grade is awesome! We're creating new businesses for Bluebonnet, reading lots of great books, and learning about the authors who wrote them. I got new medicine for my allergies and it's working! And we have tons of homework.
*Lisa, Fourth Grade*

**FIFTH GRADE:** We're at the top of the school chain, baby! Next year we're in middle school! I do like science, gathering data and stuff to draw conclusions based on experiments. That's cool.
*Fish, Fifth Grade*

**LOST AND FOUND:** Kenyan Tayler found a dirty red sweater with a hole in the sleeve on the playground. If it's yours, it's in the office.

**CAFETERIA CHAT:** The cafeteria ladies love their jobs but would not comment on the cafeteria food. I also found out that they bring their lunch.

**FROM OUR JANITOR:** Please stop sticking chewed gum under the desks.

**FROM MR. WINKY:** Yes, yes, YES!

# MYA'S ADVICE COLUMN

I'm ready to give you good advice, so drop your questions in the shoebox in the office and I will pick them up daily. Until then, my advice is, never go to bed with your boots on, and remember, there's nothing wrong with a little taradiddle every now and then!

# SPORTS

### Bluebonnet Little League Baseball

The Bluebonnet Little League baseball team lost a nail-biter to Cumberland last Saturday, 10–1. The score was tied until the last inning, when Cumberland exploded for nine runs with two outs. Bluebonnet's next game is Saturday at ten a.m. against Grimes. Come out and support the team.

# ADVERTISEMENTS

**FREE PUPPIES!** Mr. and Mrs. Rodriguez live on Fifth Street. Their dog, Chica, had five puppies that cry in English, but when they get older, they will bark in Spanish! You better hurry if you want one!

**NEW BAKERY!** The Cake Bake will give you a free cookie if you come visit. The new bakery is on Grant Street!

**GARAGE SALE! FREE STUFF!** This Saturday, Mrs. Hampton on Fourth Street is having a garage sale to get rid of all the junk in her garage. If you ask nicely, she may give you something for free!

**DJ COOL BREEZY!** Hire me for your next party! I work part-time in the produce section at Marco's Grocery. Come see me for more details.

## This Week's Fun Days

**Tuesday:** Find-a-Rainbow Day

**Wednesday:** Librarian Day

**Thursday:** Burrito Day

**Friday:** Student Athlete Day

**Saturday:** No Housework Day

## Joke of the Week

**Question:** What time is the best time to go to the dentist?

**Answer:** Tooth hurty (2:30).

# Here's a Little Taradiddle

Three Texas cowgirls made plans to ride the Oregon Trail in search of gold in the creeks and caves of California. The first cowgirl was ten years old. The second cowgirl was nine, and the third cowgirl was only four. When the horses arrived for the journey, there were only two; a big beautiful Clydesdale and a fake horse made out of a broomstick. The first cowgirl jumped on the Clydesdale and trotted off toward the Oregon Trail. The third cowgirl picked up the broomstick and trotted toward a nearby playground. But the second cowgirl didn't have a horse. At first, she was sad about being the middle cowgirl, but then she decided to start a newspaper, and yippee-ki-yay, she loves it!

# Chapter Twenty-One

Nugget and Fish can't stop talking about the *Texas Taradiddle* Special Birthday Edition as we walk home from school. Connie and I hold hands, because we know we did a good job, and we feel awesome about it.

"Everybody had a copy of the *Taradiddle*," said Nugget.

"You and Connie are famous," says Fish.

"It was almost brilliant to make the twins' and Bluebonnet's parties front-page news," says Nugget.

Connie turns around and faces my brother. "What do you mean, *almost* brilliant?"

Fish faces him, too. "Yeah! What do you mean, Nugget?"

We all laugh and keep walking. From the moment Connie and I began to sell the Special Birthday Edition up until right now, this day has been perfect. I've got an extra *ka-clink* in my *ka-clunk* as I talk about the day with Fish, Connie, and Nugget.

Soon Fish and Connie cross the street and head to their homes. I began to lose my happy feeling. It's as if crossing the street changed my mood from happy to very sad.

"I wonder if Mom's going to make us be quiet again," says Nugget.

I don't say anything because I'm trying to act like it doesn't matter to me. So I shrug.

Nugget shrugs, too. "You are really getting weird, Mya."

As soon as Nugget opens the door, we hear Macey. *"Waaaaaaaaaah! Waaaaaaaaaah!"*

Nugget heads toward the nursery. I head to my room. I still love my little sister very much, but right now, I don't want to see her. I want to be alone. I don't want to be told I can't help. I don't want to see Mom looking tired and stressed out. Today at school was one of the best days I've had in a long time. I don't want to ruin it.

In my room, I put my backpack on my desk and grab my lasso. Today is the kind of day when every cowgirl should find herself at the rodeo having boot-scootin' fun! I turn up my country and western music loud enough for me to enjoy it without anyone else hearing it.

Once I get all of my stuffed animals lined up, I lasso them one by one and then put them on my bed. When I finish, I sit on my bed and hug each animal, call it by name, and tell it that I love it so much. When I first got my stuffed animals, I hugged them all the time. Then I stopped and practiced my rodeo skills with them. I won't let that happen again.

"Mya, come eat," yells Dad.

I take my time and gently place my stuffed animals back in the drawer before going downstairs. Everybody's at the table when I get there.

"Hi," says Dad.

"Hey," I say back.

Mom's elbow is on the table, and her face sits in her hand. Her eyes blink slowly. I don't think she's going to make it all the way through dinner. Dad says the blessing, and dinner begins. Other than forks *tink*ing against plates, there's not much noise at the table. No one's talking, and what has felt uncomfortable the last two weeks now feels normal.

When I finish, I scoot back, take my plate off the table, and head toward the kitchen. Mom's asleep, and this time, Dad puts his finger to his lips for me to be quiet. He doesn't have to worry. I'm good at that.

I feel like a robot, doing what I'm told and going through the motions. But when I get to my room, I change back to my human self as I think about my day. My newspaper was the biggest thing at school, and everybody was talking about it. I don't think anything could make me come down from the clouds. Even coming home and putting the newest issue of the *Texas Taradiddle* on top of the first edition didn't bother me. Even though I can tell the first one still hadn't been read.

Once my homework is finished, I turn my music back on and try to make myself feel good by dancing. I even lip sync the songs. When that doesn't make me feel better, I try to read a book. It's a good one, where the girl finds out she's really a warrior and knows martial arts!

After an hour, I'm finished with reading. It's almost dark outside, but it's dark enough for me to close my curtains and go to bed. Normally, I would never go to bed this early. But I don't have a reason to stay up. I put on my pajamas, turn off the lights, and stare at the ceiling. I think about my little sister. I didn't see her at all today. It's not her fault that our family is broken. I'll make sure I spend time with her tomorrow. My eyes feel heavy, and I'm okay giving way to sleep.

The moment the alarm goes off, I know it's not going to be a good day. My eyes open slowly, as if they don't want to. For a few seconds, I lie there, hoping it's only a dream that the alarm went off. But I know it's not. I pull off my covers, and a sadness blankets me.

This unhappy feeling is becoming my normal one.

I sit on the edge of my bed. Rays from the sun slice through my curtains and try to make me smile, but I move my face away and get up.

I make my own ponytail this morning. It's crooked, but I don't care. Downstairs, the smell of bacon doesn't affect me at all. I notice my newspapers are still untouched.

It's hard to smile and say good morning when you're not even sure if anyone really cares. I've tried to get my parents to see how special I can be for them, but I'm doing something wrong, and I don't know what it is.

All my parents seem to do is ask me to stay quiet

as they take care of Macey. Then they make a simple dinner, watch a dumb sports show, and go to bed. I don't know what that is, but it's not the family time I'm used to. Something changed, and they didn't talk to me about it. They didn't ask me if I'd be okay with that change. They just changed it, whatever "it" was.

I get my backpack and leave without anyone noticing. I walk down the sidewalk alone. My birds aren't singing this morning. I feel them looking at me, but I can't lift my head. Maybe even the birds know I'm breaking the rule about walking to school without my brother. But I don't care.

I beat Mr. Winky to school this morning. The doors are open for early breakfast eaters, so I go in and head for the Cave. I'm sure I'll be the first person in the classroom, and that will be good because I need to get myself together.

The light is on in my classroom. Mrs. Davis is in there. Firecrackers! Maybe I can fool her, and she won't know that I've got drama. I open the door.

Mrs. Davis looks over at me and smiles. "Well, good morning, cowgirl! Are you here early to work on your next news article? What are you going to . . ."

I cover my mouth to stop the words, but I can't stop the tears. My face warms as water drips from the end of my chin, down onto my clothes. Mrs. Davis rushes to me.

"Mya, sweetie, what's going on? What happened?"

She hugs me close; I shut my eyes and pretend she's Mom. I hug tighter, and I feel her arms around me hug tighter, too. I know it's Mrs. Davis, but that's okay. It still feels wonderful to be hugged by someone I know cares about me.

"I've tried everything, Mrs. Davis, but they don't think I'm special at all. I'm not as good as Macey and Nugget."

"What are you talking about? Come sit at your desk and tell me what's going on."

"Mrs. Davis, you wouldn't happen to be a middle child, would you?"

Only the middle of her mouth opens, but I don't think she realizes it. And immediately I know I've struck gold. She nods, reaches over, and puts her hand on top of mine.

"Oh, Mya. Now everything makes sense."

For the first time in two weeks, I feel myself relax. Tears mixed with joy and pain rush down my face, and I wipe them away with my sleeve. Her face doesn't look much better than mine, and that's how I know.

I've found someone just like me.

Mrs. Davis and I sit in silence, staring at each other with this new connection.

"Mya, I know we've been working on opening new businesses in class. But is your newspaper your way of trying to get your parents' attention? The newspapers are . . . perfect. There are no spelling errors, no punctuation errors. You got stories for your paper, did the marketing for everyone, the advertising, and everything was about making sure that newspaper was awesome, which it is."

"Connie was with me every step of the way. She did a lot of the work by taking pictures, and collecting money, and even making our business plan. I also had help from Nugget and Fish. To me, the paper had to be perfect because Macey is perfectly cute, and Nugget is perfectly smart. But perfect is overrated, Mrs. Davis. A perfect newspaper didn't help me at all."

My face wrinkles as the eye faucets turn on again. Mrs. Davis hands me a tissue and responds without me saying a word.

"Mya, how many things have you done to try to get your parents to see you?"

All I can do is shrug.

"Have you spoken with your parents about how you feel?"

I shake my head and try to talk through my tears. "What am I supposed to say? I mean, it's their fault that they've forgotten about me."

"Maybe they don't realize it. When I felt left out, I talked with my parents. I'm so glad I did. I have the best relationship ever with them now. Communication is very important."

I nod, happy for Mrs. Davis that she has a good relationship with her parents. I want that. I want to be able to feel that. Talking to them is the one thing I haven't tried.

Mrs. Davis wipes her eyes. "Mya, promise me that you will talk to your parents about this. It's so important, and I know that what you're feeling is real."

I nod. "It is real. If an opportunity happens, I promise you I will talk with them."

David and Mary Frances walk in and wave. Mrs. Davis and I wave back. I feel better, and I have another plan. I'll talk to them. But if that doesn't work, I'm giving up on them.

I hug Mrs. Davis. "I'm so glad you're my teacher. Today, I wish you were my mom."

She hugs me back. "You have an amazing mom, Mya. But even when you're no longer my student, when you move on to fifth grade, I'll still be here for you if you need me."

I *ka-clunk* to the Cave and work really hard to make it through the day.

When I get home, Macey is better, not teething as much, and Mom looks more rested. But my newspapers are still sitting where I left them. Dinner is very quiet, and family time is watching the Dallas Mavericks on television. I don't want to watch the game, so I go upstairs, lasso a few animals, and think about new articles I can write for the *Texas Taradiddle*. Finally I put on my pajamas and go to bed.

As I stare at the darkness in my room, I think about what Mrs. Davis said. "Communication is very important." If Mom ever stops making me be quiet because Macey's asleep, and if Dad ever acts like he's interested, then I'll talk.

# Chapter Twenty-Two

On Thursday morning, after the pledge and our moment of silence, Mrs. Davis takes attendance and is about to tell us what to do when there's a knock on our classroom door.

It's Mr. Winky.

Who's in trouble? When our principal smiles and waves as he comes into the room, everybody seems to relax.

"Good morning, fourth graders!"

"GOOD MORNING, MR. WINKY."

"I wanted to stop by and wish each of you a wonderful day, but warn you about too much advertising of your future businesses of Bluebonnet presentations tomorrow. I was at the gas station this morning, and I heard two people talking about it, and they immediately began to ask me questions. Now don't get me wrong. I'm as proud as a papa bear, but I'm concerned about the time. Mya, I saw the note that you put in your newspaper about the business presentations being a private event. I'm not sure people are paying attention to that. I thought our agreement was that the newspaper was only to be distributed to the students and teachers. Now I think we may have a problem."

Back in October, I lassoed Naomi and got in trouble before the morning bell. Today, we just finished the pledge and our moment of silence and Mr. Winky's here, dead-eyeing me.

My face warms. Looks like I'm about to hold the record for getting busted before *and* after the bell rings. I try to explain.

"But I had to distribute the paper to everyone because I have businesses outside of school that paid me to do their marketing. I made sure I let people know that our presentations were for students, teachers, and family members. I don't see where I did anything wrong."

Mrs. Davis nods. "Mya, even though you believed

putting that note in the paper would solve every-thing, you didn't consider that some people may not pay attention to it. Yes, Mr. Winky, I had the same thoughts yesterday evening when I was in Marco's Grocery and the people behind me were talking about how excited they were about coming to see the future businesses of Bluebonnet on Friday at the school. When I turned around, they were looking at me. All I could do was smile."

Some of my classmates begin to whisper. I can't tell what they're saying, but I'm thinking it's not good. Mr. Winky continues.

"Mrs. Davis, may I speak with you in the hall for a moment?"

"Sure." She turns to us. "Class, sit quietly until I get back. I know your voices when I hear them."

As soon as the door closes, Lisa gives me a hard whisper. "What's that all about, Mya? What's Mr. Winky talking about?"

All eyes are on me as I try to explain. "It's not my fault that people don't pay attention. I think I did what Mr. Winky wanted. Listen, everybody, we need to stick to our plan. The business show goes from three o'clock until three forty-five. Then, after we all get an A for our presentations, we'll come back here and have the twins' party so that Naomi can get her A, too. We just have to be out of here before five o'clock."

Naomi tilts her head. "Why?"

"You know why. Friday is exterminator day."

"Oh, yeah, that's right," she says.

"I heard one kid got some of those exterminator chemicals on him and lost all the hair on his body. Even his eyebrows. His head looks like a ball on a pool table. And it never grew back," says Michael.

Mary Frances joins in. "I heard those chemicals are so strong that they destroy your vital organs. That's how the bugs die. It'll do the same to humans."

"I heard the exterminator sprayed a room with a bunch of lunch boxes and coats and backpacks still in it, and all that stuff had to be put in a barrel and set on fire."

Kenyan gets loud. "What are we supposed to do if we're still in the building when the exterminator comes?"

I stop the madness. "We have to make sure we're not! There's a big clock in the gym. Let's use it. We can hand out flyers and try not to get into long conversations with people. Try to keep people moving like cattle."

"We're still going to have our party, aren't we?" asks Skye.

"Nothing's going to happen, right?" asks Starr.

"It's going to be awesome," I say with a grin.

"This is the worst planning I have ever seen," says Lisa.

I feel bubbles in my guts. They're boiling. If one more person says something ugly about what I tried to do to help, I'll scream.

Johnny crosses his arms over his chest. "If we had done it ourselves, we wouldn't be in this mess. We should have never let someone else schedule our presentation times."

That's it. "Excuse me, but you weren't complaining when I told you what I did. You actually thanked me. So stop your complaining, or I will take you off the schedule and you can have your failing grade by yourself."

Naomi stands up and points at Johnny.

"Mya's right. She and Connie were just trying to help. And it's not their fault that people don't pay attention. We all saw the note in the paper about our presentations being a private event, didn't we?"

Heads nod as Naomi continues.

"We all had two whole days to look at that schedule, and we didn't figure out there was a time problem until Mr. Winky mentioned it. So if you want to be mad at someone, be mad at yourself.

And that goes for anyone else who thinks this is all Mya and Connie's fault. Instead of sitting around acting like a bunch of babies, why don't you think of a Plan B?"

Silence.

I slowly glance over my shoulder at Connie. She's got a lot of bumfuzzle in her face. I bet I do, too. The last person in the world I'd have believed would stand up for us is Naomi Jackson.

Mrs. Davis and Mr. Winky walk in and smile. Our principal nods as he looks around the room. "Very obedient students, Mrs. Davis. Yes, yes, yes. They did exactly what you told them to do. Good job. Also, we're going to continue planning for your business presentations. Tomorrow at three-thirty I will make an announcement that the presentations will be over in fifteen minutes. At exactly three-forty-five I want you cleaning up and out of the gym by four o'clock."

Mrs. Davis nods and smiles. "Well, students, I am so proud of you for staying quiet! You get an extra five minutes at recess."

While everybody is clapping, I'm staring at Naomi Jackson, my number-one enemy on the planet, who just took up for me and Connie. I look over my right shoulder at Connie. She's staring at

Naomi as if she has two heads.

What's weird is, Naomi never looks our way. She claps with everyone else over bonus recess time and listens as Mrs. Davis talk about how proud she is of us. I don't know what's going on with Naomi, but it sure is strange. Maybe I've fallen into a place where everything is backward! That would explain why Mom and Dad are ignoring me and Naomi is acting like nothing ever happened between us!

I pinch myself. It hurts. Nope. I'm really here. Mrs. Davis begins to talk.

"Mr. Winky brought up a good point. What are you going to do if you run out of time?"

"We can't run out of time because we have to have our party," says Skye.

"We have to," says Starr.

"And it's going to happen," says Naomi. "Because that's my presentation grade."

Mrs. Davis gives us all a thumbs-up. "Awesome. It sounds like everyone is confident that the time issue is not going to be a problem. I wish all of you well on that, because I can't help you. But I will tell you that Mr. Winky gets very serious about his schedule. And if you make him have to change it when he doesn't want to, you may have to suffer the consequences."

Silence.

Mrs. Davis continues. "Okay, now that we've got that handled, let's talk about tomorrow. Our janitor is going to set up some individual tables in the gymnasium for you to do your presentations. I will be roaming through the crowds of people, watching your interactions and their reactions to your products. I will grade you on how courteous you are, how informative you are about your product, and how people respond to your presentation."

"Do we have to dress up?"

I decide to give one back to Naomi, since she took up for me. "Dress for the twins' party. Naomi said we're supposed to wear black and white, remember?"

Heads nod, and "oh yeahs" are heard through the classroom.

Excitement begins to rise again. Everyone is talking at the same time. The room is back to normal.

But I know there's nothing normal about this situation. If our presentations and the twins' party don't go as planned, Connie and I will get blamed, and I'll spend the rest of my life trying to apologize to my classmates, especially the twins, for messing up this very important day.

## Chapter Twenty-Three

In the Cave, everybody's wearing black and white for the twins' party. There are a few decorations up, but nothing will ever top the big banner that reads HAPPY BIRTHDAY, SKYE & STARR that's taped across the wall near their cabinet. Everybody's taking turns wishing them a happy birthday.

The twins are rockin' brand-new black-and-white striped pants with black T-shirts covered in silver glitter. Mary Frances has on a pretty black dress with a white collar. Lisa has on a black skirt with a white blouse. Connie has on her white blouse with the black skulls all over it. She even drew a bunch of white skulls on her black shorts. I'm wearing a black jean skirt and a white blouse with fringe hanging from the arms and the pockets. I feel different not having my pink boots on, but I want the twins' party to be perfect. I've got a pair of white Skechers on that I don't wear very often. They are perfect for today.

The guys have on black pants and white shirts. Even Mrs. Davis has on a black-and-white dress! Everybody looks so nice! Maybe I was wrong about these fancy-schmancy parties. There's a pile of presents near the twins' cabinets. Naomi moves them to a big open space on the other side of the room. She's got on a beautiful white dress with a black sash that she probably wore during a beauty pageant. But still, she looks beautiful.

The bell rings, and we all rush to our seats. Mrs. Davis gives us an evil eye, but then smiles because she knows we're all so excited. I look around the room. It looks so clean with all the white shirts! Spring is definitely in our classroom today.

After what feels like forty hours, it's time to go to lunch, and then recess. We keep rushing to the fence, hoping to catch a glimpse of someone bringing something in for the twins' party. Naomi walks around with Starr and Skye as if she's their host for the whole day.

I'm sure Naomi's going to move up the friendship list for the twins after this. I wonder if she'll move past me. This is a really big deal, and I would have never thought of doing something so awesome. I hear Mrs. Davis calling for Naomi, and they both disappear into the school. This must be it. The cake and food must be here. We're about to get our party on!

Nugget walks over to the twins. "Happy birthday, Skye and Starr."

Fish does the same. "Happy birthday! Don't forget to save me a piece of cake!"

We're all disappointed when we return from recess and none of the goodies are in the Cave. Naomi keeps looking at the clock. I bet she's nervous. This is not only her presentation grade, but a real party for two of the most popular students in the whole school!

Later that afternoon, it's hard not to notice all the cars lining up at the curb, even when I'm supposed to be listening to Mrs. Davis. I check the clock. Two thirty-five.

"Mya, are you paying attention?" asks Mrs. Davis.

I can't lie to her. "Those can't be for the presentations today, can they?"

"I think they are," she says.

My heart pounds harder as my classmates check out the line of cars outside.

"Oh no," says Kenyan. "I better cut my cookies in fours, or I'll never have enough."

"I'm glad I bought tiny cups for my Jungle Juice," says Johnny.

"It doesn't even start for almost another half hour," says Michael.

"Did anybody think of a Plan B? I think we're going to need it," says Lisa.

Connie stands and tries to get everyone to repeat after her. "Work fast, talk fast, keep the line moving. Work fast, talk fast, keep the line moving."

It's a chant until someone knocks on the door and then opens it. "Excuse me, I have a delivery for Naomi Jackson? It's a really big cake and party supplies!"

Everybody stands to try to see the cake. Skye and Starr run to the front of the class to walk the delivery person into the Cave.

He smiles at the twins. "I've got lots more to bring in. This party starts at three, right?"

"We've moved it to three forty-five," says Naomi as she tries to check things off her list while he's bringing them in. There's balloons, plates, napkins, forks, an ice chest with drinks in it, and another ice chest with ice cream.

"I'll be back to pick up these ice chests on Monday morning. Leave them in here, and I'll stop by before school starts," says the delivery guy.

Naomi gives him two thumbs up. Starr and Skye hug him.

Skye hollers out, "Hey, everybody, you've got to come see our cake! It's beautiful!"

I'm trying to get into the Cave as quickly as everybody else. This is a big deal, and so far, everything is going great. Naomi has a big grin on her face, and the twins are happy.

There's lots of ooohs and ahhhs before I see it. When I do, I totally get why everyone's making such a fuss. Skye stands on one side of the cake. Starr stands on the other.

"Look at this, Mya. It's perfect," says Skye.

"So perfect," says Starr.

And it is. On the cake is a picture of a forest at night with a very black sky. White coyotes howl at the moon, a black tree has a white owl in it, and there are white stars all over the horizon that spell HAPPY BIRTHDAY, SKYE AND STARR.

Mrs. Davis steps inside the cave. "Okay, class, I agree. That is a beautiful cake, and it's perfect for two of our favorite students, Skye and Starr. But we have presentations to do, and the doors open in the gym soon. I suggest you get your products, set up your tables, and prepare to represent the future business world of Bluebonnet!"

Work becomes fun, even helping the janitor put up tables. We listen to each other's presentations and help make the tables look nice. I feel very close to my classmates right now as we get ready to show off our talents. It's three o'clock, and the doors are open.

The gym is packed, and people are still trying to get in. Things are going well, but I'm beginning to worry about the time. I look at the clock above the basketball hoop.

Three twenty-five.

Mr. Winky has to be making that announcement soon. Mrs. Davis is still taking pictures. Kenyan is hanging a sign that reads I DON'T HAVE ANY MORE COOKIES. Johnny's out of Jungle Juice, and it all happened in the first twenty minutes!

An older couple walks up to me. "Tell us about your newspaper, the *Texas Taradiddle*."

I begin to explain, but in the middle of my talk, the old man interrupts me. "We used to tell taradiddles all the time back on the ranch. Must have been fifty years ago! Yes, I was just a boy living in Fort

Worth, working as a ranch hand. We had hundreds of acres with longhorn cows, and we even had a few buffalo. I saw that word taradiddle, and it brought back memories of working on the ranch. Good luck with your newspaper, young ladies."

Connie and I both thank him. As I try to leave our table, a lady puts her hand on my shoulder. "I'm really glad to see our young girls getting involved in the business world. We've been kept out of it for so long. I'm rooting for you, honey! Long live the *Texas Taradiddle*!"

"Thank you," I say.

I check the clock again. Three thirty-five. Where is Mr. Winky? He said he would make an announcement for people to leave, but I haven't heard anything. I look around the room and see Naomi talking with DJ Cool Breezy! Holy moly, that guy is so cute! But I know he's here for the twins' party, and before that can happen, I've got to go make this event come to an end!

I notice the twins telling a lady that in her past life, she lived in Virginia, was a soldier for the Confederate army, and made chocolate fudge for the governor. The lady seems delighted!

There's Mr. Winky, over by Susan's homemade chips and dips. He's laughing and talking to a group of adults as they eat at Susan's table. I race over and tug on his coat sleeve.

"Mr. Winky, I thought you were going to make an announcement?"

"Oh, yes, yes, yes, Mya. And by the way, this was such a wonderful idea! There are so many people here, including members of the school board! They love this. So I decided to give your class extra time, and I told the exterminator that, instead of starting in the gymnasium, he can begin spraying in some of the classrooms far from the gym. That way, if he gets here a little early, he doesn't have to wait around for us to finish. But we have to be gone by five."

"Oh, yes, sir," I say, holding back tears.

Good gravy in the navy! We've got to get out of this gym and back to our classroom! The twins' party is supposed to start in fifteen minutes, and DJ Cool Breezy is already here, waiting to set up. Naomi is going to flip out if she isn't able to get a grade for her presentation. But even worse, the twins deserve this party, and we can't let them down.

I go to each one of my classmates and whisper, "Talk faster, and tell people we're about to shut this down so they should leave to avoid the traffic. If we don't, we'll miss the birthday party. Tell them whatever you want, but we have to get them to leave!"

I check the clock again.

Ten minutes before four o'clock.

The gym is still packed, and there are more people coming in. My classmates are calling to me, but I can't answer them right now because I don't have an answer. I don't know what to do. I'm scared to look at the twins, because I'm sure they're freaking out. I've got to do something, and I better do it in a hurry. Mr. Winky and the school-board members are laughing and talking so loud that some people stop to look at them.

Wait a minute. I've got an idea.

I tell Connie first. "I'm going to do the announcement over the intercom."

Connie's breathing changes from normal to fast. She looks around the room as if I told her I'd stolen a million dollars. Then she whispers to me, "You could get in a lot of trouble, Mya."

"I don't have any other choice. It's either stay in here and the twins don't get to have their birthday party, or make an announcement and maybe, we'll get to party for about ten minutes before we have to go."

Connie moves her hair behind her ears and wipes her forehead with the back of her hand. "Oh my gosh, this is terrible. Please, Mya, don't get caught."

I dash away to the office. The door is open, so I tiptoe over to the broadcasting room, in case Mr. Winky's secretary is still here. The room is dark, and I choose not to turn on any lights. I use the lights from the office. I'm not completely sure how to use this equipment, so I just start flipping switches. Suddenly a light comes on that says ON AIR. I stand in front of the microphone and try to speak in a voice that doesn't sound like mine so no one will recognize me.

"Ladies and gentlemen, thank you for coming to Bluebonnet's future business presentations, but we have to go. So please begin to exit the building in a quiet and orderly fashion. We'll see everybody at the park next week! Thank you, and good night!"

As I turn to open the door, there's Mr. Winky, glaring through the window in the door. He's not smiling as he signals me to come out.

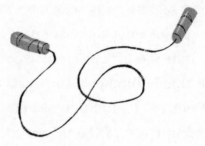

# Chapter Twenty-Four

"Mr. Winky, it was getting scary in the gym, and . . . and there were too many people . . . and . . . and I was thinking that maybe—"

He interrupts me. "Go sit in my office, Mya. I'll be there in a moment."

It's over. I'm done. I've failed in a big way. I'm so frustrated that I lose my mind and holler at Mr. Winky.

"You're making a big mistake! They're going to miss their party!"

He stops for a moment but doesn't turn around to look at me before walking away. I burst into tears as I step into his office. What was I thinking? I've never yelled at Mr. Winky! That makes him the second adult I've hollered at in the last couple of weeks. What's happening to me? Am I turning into that girl Connie went to school with? Maria Escobar?

I barely make it to one of the office chairs before collapsing into it. Two minutes later, Mr. Winky shows up. I look at the clock.

Twenty minutes after four.

Mr. Winky starts in on me. "Mya, do you enjoy going to in-school detention?"

"No, sir."

"Then why would you use school equipment without permission? That's almost the equivalent of trespassing. What do you have to say for yourself?"

I don't even know where to start. And at that moment, it doesn't seem worth it to try. So I stay silent.

Mr. Winky sits behind his desk. "I can't lie to you, Mya. I'm very shocked by your behavior. I guess I shouldn't be, after you lassoed a girl last fall. But still, this is unacceptable. Report to my office at eight o'clock Monday morning for a full day of in-school detention."

"Yes, sir. And I'm sorry, if that helps any. I'm not going to argue about my punishment, because

I deserve it. May I go now?"

"Yes, you may."

As I turn to leave Mr. Winky's office, I see Mrs. Davis waiting patiently outside his door. I hope she hasn't come to tear into me, too. But when I open the door, she smiles and looks directly at my principal.

"May I have a word with you, Mr. Winky?"

"Sure, sure, come on in."

Before going in, Mrs. Davis bends down and hugs me. "I've told all your classmates to leave for the day. I'll get the cake and party supplies out of the Cave. We'll figure something else out on Monday. Go home, Mya. Talk to your parents."

"No, Mrs. Davis! You have to come back to our classroom and give Naomi a grade for her presentation! We still have a few minutes before five o'clock. Please!"

"But Mya, I told your classmates to go home."

"Trust me, Mrs. Davis. They're still here. Come on, we have to hurry!"

She holds up one finger. "I'll be right back, Mr. Winky."

It's strange running down a hall with a teacher. That's against every rule on the planet. But it's happening right now as Mrs. Davis and I dash down the hall toward our classroom. Behind me, lots of voices blend together, screaming at each other to hurry. It's my classmates.

All of us, including Mrs. Davis, keep going. Shoes screech on the tile as we cut the corner like Olympians. Naomi and Connie catch up to me. We're running together, leading the way with Mrs. Davis. I hear the twins behind us.

"We're going to make it," says Skye.

"We've got to make it," says Starr.

The panic in their voices makes me weak. But when we reach our classroom, and I look through the glass in the door, all the air inside me leaves. There's somebody in there, and it's not DJ Cool Breezy.

He's got a big white hat over his head and face. There's a window on the face part so he can see. A white jumpsuit, with white boots and white gloves, makes it easy to recognize who he is. We beat on the window of the door, but he can't hear us.

Suddenly he takes three steps toward the Cave, spraying everything on the left and right.

"NOOOOOO!!!"

Skye begins to cry. "Make him stop, Starr."

"I can't make him stop," cries Starr.

Naomi's crying, too. All of her work, and she doesn't even get a grade for it!

"Okay, everyone, let's just calm down and take a breath. We can come up with another plan," says Mrs. Davis.

The exterminator disappears into the Cave, spraying the walls, the ceiling, the floor, everything.

Mrs. Davis continues, "I know everyone's disappointed, especially the twins. And I feel horrible that this happened."

Suddenly the exterminator rushes out and looks around. He spots us at the door and heads our way. Johnny yells, waving his hands in the air.

"HE'S COMING WITH THE CHEMICALS! RUN FOR YOUR LIVES!"

We scatter like rodents, running toward the exit doors. Once we're outside, someone starts counting to make sure we all made it out alive. There are other students from school outside, asking us what happened. Lisa's out of breath as she tells them.

"Our backpacks and jackets are still in there," says David.

Mary Frances shakes her head. "But they're in our cabinets, so they're safe."

I'm still bent over from running when I hear the saddest sound I've heard in a long time. The twins hold each other and cry so hard that I can feel it inside me. I begin to cry, too, because I wanted their birthday party to be incredible. And it's my fault that it didn't happen.

"I'm so sorry, Skye and Starr."

"Our cake," says Skye.

"No cake for us," says Starr.

"You really blew this one, Mya," says Johnny.

"Yeah, this is bad," says Michael.

"Shut up! Just shut up!" yells Lisa.

"You don't tell me to shut up," says Michael.

"Calm down," says Mary Frances.

"Easy for you to say! It wasn't your birthday party!" yells Johnny.

I can't take it. It's too much. I've ruined everything.

*Run, Mya. Run away!*

I listen to the little voice inside me and dash down the street.

"Mya, come back!"

I hear them calling me, but I keep running. Three words keeps clogging my thoughts, and I can't make them go away.

*You're not special. You're not special.*

I run home and hide in the backyard, in the little shed where Dad keeps his lawn mower and tools. No one will look for me here. I'm crying so hard that I can't catch my breath. The shed is quiet, as if everything in it is listening to me. I whisper and cry at the same time.

"What have I done? I ruined everything. Skye and Starr, I am so sorry. I would never do anything to hurt you. I wanted your party to be perfect. I wanted that more than anything. You have to believe me."

I stop crying, lean against the lawn mower, and go to sleep.

Crickets are loud. I never knew how loud they could be when it's getting dark outside.

Good gravy in the navy! It's dark in here!

I get up, open the shed, and look through the back-door window. I spot Mom on the phone, and Dad's pacing, while Nugget paces beside him. I don't see Macey.

I knock on the back door. I know I'm going to be in big trouble. Why should that bother me? My whole day has been nothing but trouble. I wonder if they ate dinner without me. Did they even hear me knock?

I see my brother looking. He hollers that I'm at the back door. Dad rushes and opens it as Mom comes, still talking on the phone. I hear her say. "Never mind, she just walked in. Thanks anyway. Goodbye."

Dad has a strong grip on my arm as he pulls me into the house. "Where have you been?"

"In the shed. I woke up when I heard the crickets."

"Do you know how badly you scared us?"

"I'm sorry. It was an accident."

"I got a call from Mr. Winky. He said you have in-school detention on Monday for using the school intercom without permission. What's that all about, Mya? You know better than that! You promised your mom and me that you would stay out of trouble!"

I tell him the truth. "It was something I had to do."

Dad stares at me a long time. "Go get washed up for dinner."

"Yes, sir."

Mom and Nugget stand next to each other and watch me climb the stairs as if I've never done it before. I don't take long in the bathroom because I don't want any more trouble. I've had enough in one day to last me six years. I get downstairs and take my place at the table, but something's wrong. I can feel it. It's as if my body is shaking, and it's waiting for the right time to explode.

I've got to stay under control.

# Chapter Twenty-Five

We're sitting at the table, waiting on Dad, when Nugget goes berserk.

"It's already all over the neighborhood what happened after school. I can't believe you guys blew the twins' party. And you hijacked the intercom? Unbelievable. I'm sure Naomi had a lot to do with it," says Nugget.

"Stop talking about her like that," I say.

"I'm glad you're not friends with her anymore," he says.

Mom rolls her eyes. "Okay, I think that's being . . ."

"And what if I was?" I ask, staring him in the

face. My body's shaking more and more.

"I can't even begin to say how embarrassed I would be as your brother to say that you were my sister and still hanging out with Phony Naomi."

I lean across the table and explode. "You've got a lot of nerve! You have no idea how many times I've had to explain that your head was always shaped that way. And I still claimed you! I was with you when you dumped your perfectly good best friend, Fish, for that rotten, no-good Solo Grubb, remember?"

Nugget yells, "There is absolutely nothing wrong with the shape of my head!"

I yell back. "You'll probably marry a chicken tender!"

Nugget's voice softens as he threatens me. "Cut it out, Mya! I mean it!"

I'm still yelling. "Go to McDonald's and order a bucket of nuggets so you'll know what your babies' heads are going to look like when you get married!"

Dad's voice echoes off the walls. "NUGGET! MYA! STOP IT!"

"*Waaaaaaaaaah! Waaaaaaaaaah!*"

"Great. I was hoping to get a quick nap after dinner while she was still asleep. Thanks a lot," says Mom.

Dad closes his eyes and then puts up his hands as he speaks to Mom. "Honey, grab Macey and meet me in the backyard."

Mom leaves, and I notice Dad's face has a whole lot of mad in it. He's breathing like Buttercup, our mechanical bull that we keep at our store. Dad speaks softer, but what he says makes me nervous.

"Nugget, Mya, go to the backyard and sit at the picnic table until I get there! Do not talk to each other, and once you sit down, you'd better not move!"

My Skechers make screeching noises across the floor as I make my way to the backyard, madder than a wet cat! I don't know what Dad wants to show us or say to us in the backyard, but he better hurry, because I'm ready to rip Nugget's face off.

I sit on one side of the picnic table and my brother sits on the other. I can't believe he said I embarrassed him. I'm about to open my mouth and zing him again when Mom comes out of the house with Macey in her arms. She doesn't sit at the picnic table with us. Instead, she parks in a lounge chair not far from the back door. Soon Dad comes out of the garage with a handful of stuff.

"Nugget, Mya, get over here," he says.

He gives us five nails and a hammer each, and then points at a spot on our fence.

"I want you to imagine that each piece of wood on our fence is a person. Go hammer all of your nails into one of those pieces of wood."

"Why?" asks Nugget.

"Because he told us to," I say.

"I can answer for myself, young lady," says Dad.

It takes less than two minutes for Nugget and me to hammer those nails into the fence. We walk back to Dad and try to give him the hammers. He won't take them.

"Look at the nails in the wood. See them?"

"Yes, sir," we say.

"Good. I want you to imagine that those are hurtful things that you've said or done to someone."

I stare at the nails in the fence, and for a moment, I think of the twins. It hurts me to know that I caused that kind of pain for them. Dad points at the fence again.

"Now use the other side of your hammer and take out all of those nails that you just hammered in."

I'm ready to scream! What is Dad doing? I shrug at him, and ask the obvious question.

"We just hammered them in! Now you want us to take them out? That doesn't make sense."

He answers me with his eyes and one-word sentences.

"Go. Do. It. Now."

Nugget and I mumble as we pull the nails from the fence and bring them back to Dad. He takes the nails and points at the fence.

"Taking the nails out of the fence represents you saying 'I'm sorry.'"

That makes me feel a little better, because that is exactly what I intend to do to Skye and Starr. But Dad says something I wasn't expecting.

"Okay. Even though the nails are out, look at the fence. There are holes there. That's because when you say something ugly or do something bad to someone, it can leave a painful hole in them, like a scar, even after you say 'I'm sorry.' Sometimes saying 'I'm sorry' is not enough. Words hurt."

Dad picks up two small trays with gray gooey stuff in them. There's a tool with it that looks like something that could spread icing on a really big cake.

"Take these trays of wood putty and a spreader. Go fill those holes."

I'm on it. As quickly as I can, I spread that wood putty across the holes. I put it on thick, making sure all of the holes are completely covered before taking the supplies back to Dad. I'm thinking that was a good lesson, and maybe I should even apologize to my brother because I don't want to leave holes in anyone. But before I can say anything, Dad messes my head up again.

"Now look at the fence. You covered up the holes, but it doesn't look like it did before you put the nails in, does it?"

I look at the gray gooey stuff covering the holes. The fence doesn't look nearly as nice as it did before. I keep staring at it as Dad continues.

"When you say hurtful things to people, or do mean things, those people you hurt are never the same."

Tears roll down my face as I turn to Nugget. "Sorry for the holes I put in you, Nugget."

"I'm sorry for scarring you up, Mya."

Mom comes and stands next to Dad as he continues.

"We're family, and if there's a problem, we should talk it out like family. How would you feel if your mother and I treated you like you treat each other?"

Nugget shrugs, but I'm shaking, knowing I need to speak up. The words are right on the tip of my tongue, but they won't come out.

"So live your lives so that you don't have to do this exercise again," says Mom.

That does it. Either I'm about to be in worse

trouble than I was ten minutes ago, or I'm going to get sent to my room for the rest of my life. But I believe what Mrs. Davis told me. I've got to let them know, and the words fall out of my mouth like I'm throwing up.

"Is that exercise for you and Dad, too?"

"Of course," says Mom.

"Do you know how many holes you and Dad have put in me?"

Silence.

Mom's eyebrows come closer together. "What are you talking about, Mya? We have not said one ugly thing to you."

The tears are streaming down my face. "You haven't hardly said one thing, period. And you haven't done anything with me, either. Dad, you take Nugget to the store and teach him everything about inventory lists and stuff like that. Mom, you don't even let me help you in the kitchen anymore. You don't ask me if I need help with my homework. You barely talk to me when you're braiding my hair in the morning. And when I come home in the afternoon, you don't even have time to hear about my day. You just tell me to be quiet because Macey's asleep."

Dad tries to interrupt me. "Mya, sweetheart . . ."

"No! Let me finish! I need to get this out of me

because if you want to imagine that I'm one of those pieces of wood, you have to know that I've still got the nails in me. You haven't even apologized."

Dad scratches his head and bites his bottom lip. I keep talking.

"It's as if I'm invisible to you. All you seem to care about are Nugget and Macey. You totally forgot that I'm your daughter, too. I don't know what else to do to get you to see me."

"We see you and cherish you, Mya," says Dad.

"That can't be true, because if it was, the newspaper that I worked so hard on to please you wouldn't still be sitting on the coffee table where I left it one week ago, when you promised me you'd read it. You let it sit there so long that there's now two different copies! A first edition and a Special Birthday Edition. Being a middle child is the worst thing that can happen to anybody."

Mom bursts into tears. Dad's eyes water. It doesn't matter.

As fast as my Skechers can carry me, I run again, like I did at school. This time I grab my backpack at the front door and then take the stairs two at a time until I reach my room. I shut my bedroom door, lock it, and stretch out across my bed, hugging my pillow. I don't remember ever crying this hard. I can't remember when I felt so hurt and alone.

*Knock, knock, knock.*

"Mya, it's Dad. Can I come in?"

"I just want to be alone right now."

"But you haven't eaten dinner. We ordered pizza because dinner is cold."

"I'm not hungry. I'm going to bed."

Silence.

His voice trails off. "Okay. I'll see you in the morning. . . ."

I listen to Dad's footsteps as he leaves. I roll over and wipe my face. The nails and wood putty are still on my mind. I wonder how much wood putty I have on my heart. It sure hurts, but tonight, by telling my parents how I feel, I think I made a step in the right direction.

# Chapter Twenty-Six

It's quiet at the breakfast table. None of the usual sounds of papers ruffling or turning. I *ka-clunk* in to see Dad and Nugget eating breakfast. The *Bluebonnet Tribune* is still rolled up with a rubber band around it. Dad's talking to Nugget, but then he smiles when he sees me.

"Hey, baby girl," he says.

I can't help but smile.

"What's wrong?" Dad asks.

"You stopped calling me baby girl and gave that name to Macey. It's just . . . I'm glad to hear you call me that again."

Dad runs his hand across his face and through his hair. "I can't believe I lost touch with you that fast. I'm so glad you talked to us, Mya."

"I think it may have been the corn prices," I say.

Dad shakes his head. "No excuses."

I take my seat at the table. "Good morning,"

Mom puts a plate of fruit, yogurt, and biscuits in front of me. Then she kisses me on the forehead. I cut my eyes toward my brother, and he's smiling.

Okay, who are these people, and what did they do with my real family that's ignored me over the past two weeks? "Where's Macey?" I ask.

Mom nods her head toward the nursery. "She's been fed, her diaper's changed, and she's listening to nursery-rhyme songs. So I left her in the little baby rocker bed while I spend these few moments with you and Nugget on this beautiful Saturday morning. And soon, we're going to have a family meeting. I promise you that everything is going to be fine. How many braids today?"

"Five."

Mom puts her hands on her hips and grins. "And exactly why do you want five?"

"One for each member of my family."

I'm face-to-face with Mom, and there's no doubt

in my mind that she sees me, and I'm feeling special. It doesn't matter that it's Saturday and I don't have anywhere to go. I want to stand up and do the Mya Shuffle! This is exactly what I wanted. I needed my parents to remember that they have three kids, not two.

After breakfast, Nugget and I head outside. Soon, Fish joins us.

"When's the next newspaper coming, Mya Papaya?"

"I don't know. I need to talk with more people first."

Fish grins. "Okay. So Nugget, you want to play some catch at the field?"

"Yeah, let me get my glove."

Soon Nugget and Fish are on their bikes, heading to the baseball fields. I'm sitting on the porch, wondering what I can do. I'm sure no one wants to hang out with me. I rest my elbows on my knees, hold my face in the palms of my hands, and stare at the ground.

Suddenly a pair of pink tennis shoes appears with a pair of feet in them. I look up.

"Hey, Naomi. What are you doing here?"

"I know that you and the twins have been friends

a long time. Longer than I've been friends with them. I thought maybe they'd listen to you before they'd listen to me."

What the what? Did Naomi just tell the truth? That should go in the next edition of the *Texas Taradiddle*.

"Listen to me about what?" I ask.

"Do you think you can get them to the park next Saturday during Bluebonnet's birthday bash?"

I shrug. "Why?"

"Maybe we can still have their party. But I can't afford to buy another big cake like that one they had yesterday. I've used up all the money Mr. and Mrs. Falling gave to me to plan the party. I totally failed as a party planner."

I stare at the ground. "Yeah, that was pretty bad. I don't want to talk about it."

"Me either. So let's work together on making it right for the twins."

That doesn't sound like the Naomi Jackson who I know. A red flag pops into my head. "Why are you asking me to help you? How do I know you're not setting me up?"

"Because I'm not."

I stand and deadeye her. "It seems weird that

you would all of a sudden come asking me for help."

Naomi grins her evil grin. "Get over yourself, Mya. I'm not here for you. I'm here for the twins. I know you care about them as much as I do. I'm willing to put my drama with you aside until we fix this for Skye and Starr. Are you in or not? I don't have all day."

That sounds like Naomi, but what she says next takes me by surprise.

"Wait, hold on a minute. I didn't mean that, Mya. I . . . I've been trying to change the way I talk to people. I meant what I said about the twins, but I didn't mean what I said about you getting over yourself, and all that other rude stuff."

Holy moly! I twirl my braids with my fingers because I don't know what else to do. I hope she's telling the truth. I'm going to believe her. Maybe because I want to.

"Okay, Naomi. I'm in. Let me say that I'm not good at making cakes. And my mom is pretty busy with Macey, so she wouldn't have time to help me."

Naomi nods. "Same here. Mom's personal party planner business is really busy. You mind if I sit down on your porch while we think?"

I scoot over, and Naomi sits next to me. We're not

talking, but it's for a good reason. I know we're both thinking as hard as we can.

"Skye and Starr's parents paid over a hundred dollars for that cake. They said they will not buy another one."

"Connie and I made seventy bucks from selling newspapers and advertisements. We bought three more reams of paper, a stapler, and some staples. That leaves us with less than forty bucks. Not even close to a hundred dollars."

Naomi shakes her head. "I'd settle for a couple boxes of cookies from the Cake Bake instead of a cake. Maybe that nice lady who owns it will throw in a gallon of milk for free."

I nod. "The Cake Bake? I'd take Kenyan's cookies and Johnny's Jungle Juice if . . . wait a minute."

Naomi looks my way. "What?"

I rush to the front door. "Don't move. I'll be right back."

I run to the coffee table to grab a copy of the *Texas Taradiddle*. Both copies are gone.

Even though I'm happy that Mom and Dad have my newspapers, I really need a copy right now. I dash to my room, grab one, and race back to Naomi on the porch. She's standing, eyes wide open and hands folded across her chest. I'm out of breath.

She gets to the point.

"Okay, so what's the big plan, Mya?"

I show her the advertisement page of the *Texas Taradiddle*. "Have you paid attention to all the businesses that our class was going to open? Cupcakes, cookies, Jungle Juice, chips and dips, that's party food! *We* can make the twins' party happen on their birthday. There can be the big party going on for Bluebonnet, and a little party going on for the twins at the same time!"

"Boom! Hello, Plan B. Let's put that together for the twins," she says.

"For the twins," I say back. "Thanks, Naomi."

I'm freaking, listening to her sound like my old friend. I can't help it. I have to ask her.

"Naomi?"

She turns around. "Yeah?"

"Do you . . . I mean . . . have you ever thought about our friendship? I mean, do you miss it?"

She nods. "Every day. So please, I don't want to lose the twins as my friends, too."

"If that's true, then why did you give me that ugly nickname, and treat me mean?"

Naomi turns away from me and faces the sidewalk. She doesn't speak right away, but when she does, I can't believe what she says. "This is very hard for me, Mya, because I've never seriously apologized for anything. My parents have made me say sorry before, but that doesn't mean I meant it."

"So why should I believe you now?" I ask.

"Because there's nobody here making me say it. I decided on my own to stop calling you Mya Tibbs Fibs, and I hoped that I'd get a chance to say . . . I'm really sorry for everything I've said and done to you. Mya, you were the best friend I ever had. Connie is really lucky to have you."

Good gravy in the buckeye navy.

My whole body tingles like it's Christmas morning, or maybe my birthday. Naomi and I are zoned in, staring at each other in complete silence. I want to tell her all over again how I really wanted to be her Spirit Week partner, and how I loved being her best friend, and how much it hurt me when she dissed me. I want to tell her so many things, but right now, I don't think she needs to hear that. Before I can say anything, Naomi leans against the house.

"Hopefully one day soon, you, Connie, and I will be able to sit down and talk things out. But first, let's make sure the twins' party happens."

I smile. "Don't worry. It will. But I've got in-school detention on Monday."

Naomi puts her hands on her hips. "Who'd you lasso?"

We both laugh, and then I tell her what happened.

"Okay, so you'll have to figure out a way to help me get the word out next week."

# Chapter Twenty-Seven

I've got a *ka-clunk* in my walk that's so good I can snap my fingers to it! No one would figure out that I'm on my way to in-school detention as soon as I get to school. But today, that could be a plus. I need extra time to think things out and help Naomi make this the best party ever. I wonder if she talked to Connie. Probably not. Connie hates her.

But I spot my best friend standing by the flag-pole waiting for me like she does sometimes. I wave and trot over to meet her.

"You'll never guess who came to my house this weekend."

Connie shrugs. "Who?"

"Me," says a voice behind me.

It's Naomi. She's by herself. Connie lets out a big sigh. She rolls her eyes and looks away. But she doesn't leave, even when Naomi starts talking.

"Mya, don't forget that you've got to figure out a way to make the twins come to the park on Saturday. I know you can't today, but don't forget."

"I won't," I say.

And then Naomi says something that almost makes me cry.

"Connie, I know you hate my guts, but I really need to make this party happen for the twins. I know you love Skye and Starr as much as Mya and I do. Can we just put our drama aside and try to give them a really good party?"

Connie nods, but I can tell she's not ready to trust Naomi yet. And I understand. I hope Naomi does, too. She continues to talk.

"Mya said she has detention all day, but she came up with a really good Plan B for the twins' party."

Connie agrees. "Fine. I'll help. But for the record, Jackson, I'm only doing this for the twins."

Connie refuses to call Naomi by her first name. If she doesn't like a person, she calls them by their last name. She called me Tibbs until she got to know me.

"Good. I'll be in touch." And with that, Naomi walks away.

Connie and I walk together toward the door. When Mr. Winky sees me, he points to his office. "Good morning to Bluebonnet's favorite cowgirl who turned villain last Friday. And good morning to Bluebonnet's youngest Picasso! Mya, to my office. Connie, to class. Yes, yes, yes. It's going to be a beautiful day at Young Elementary School."

I try not to laugh, because I'm too happy to care about the punishment right now. I know I was wrong, and I'll never do that again. But to have Connie and potentially Naomi as friends is way better than sitting in a room by myself all day.

Mrs. Davis comes and takes me to the detention room. She gives me a little lecture about controlling my behavior, and then she's gone. I've got books to read, and homework to do, so I get to it. Ten minutes later, I'm bored.

I try to sing, but it doesn't make me feel any better. I get up and do the Mya Shuffle. Now this is fun! I sing and dance until I hear someone clear their throat.

"I brought you this week's spelling words. Mrs. Davis forgot to give them to you."

David puts the paper on the desk with my other

books. "So what was that dance you were doing?"

"It's one I made up. It's called the Mya Shuffle."

"It's cool. Can you teach me?"

"Are you going to steal it?"

"No! I'm going to teach it, and call it the Mya Tibbs Shuffle. Can't get any more obvious than that, Mya."

I giggle and, right there in detention, teach David my dance. He catches on quickly, and soon we're adding other things to the shuffle to make it more fun.

"I'd better go before I end up in here, too. Naomi and Connie are talking about a redo of the twins' party on Saturday. I'm down. You coming?"

"Of course!"

"Okay. We could all do the Mya Shuffle at the party! That would be boo-yang! Later, Mya."

"Bye."

It's lunchtime, and I'm ready to eat. Mrs. Davis should be walking in with my lunch tray any minute now. There's a knock, and then the door opens. But it's not Mrs. Davis.

"Hi, Mya," says Skye.

"Hi, Mya," says Starr.

They're both dressed in all black, like somebody died. I try not to cry as they come in. Skye's carrying a tray with my plate and napkin on it. Starr has a carton of milk and an apple.

This is the first time I've seen them since Friday afternoon when we all ran from the exterminator. I haven't called them. I haven't gone to their house. I've been so ashamed, and I couldn't face them. Now, I don't have any choice.

"Hi. Uh, thanks for bringing my lunch."

"We know why you're in here, Mya," says Skye.

"We know why," says Starr.

"You were trying to make our party happen," says Skye.

"You tried so hard, Mya," says Starr.

I can't take it. "I'm so sorry. You should have had an amazing party, but I made a really big mistake by trying to schedule everything at the same time, and then inviting the whole town to come. You have no idea how awful I feel."

"It's okay, Mya. Don't feel awful," says Skye.

"Don't feel awful," says Starr.

"We still love you," says Skye.

"You're our very first friend, and we love you," says Starr.

An idea flashes across my brain. I know it's low-down, but I have to use whatever I can to help me.

"If it's true that you love me, then you'll come to

the park on Saturday for the Bluebonnet party."

Skye shakes her head. "We love you, but we won't be there, Mya."

"We won't be there," says Starr.

"We're still very sad, and not in the mood to party with others right now," says Skye.

"We don't want to go to somebody else's party right now," says Starr.

I wasn't expecting that answer. *Think, Mya.*

"Macey's going to be a Bluebonnet flower with a bunch of other babies. They're going to be a flower garden. You've got to come see her."

Starr and Skye hold hands.

"Awww, Macey's going to be a flower?" asks Skye.

"A bluebonnet flower?" asks Starr.

"You've got to come and take pictures with her," I say.

"We'll definitely be there," says Skye.

"Definitely," says Starr.

"Perfect. Try to be at the park by ten, okay? Then you'll get the best pictures."

"Okay," says Skye.

"We'll be there at ten," says Starr.

Skye puts my tray on an empty desk. Starr puts my apple and milk on the tray before they both wave and leave.

I stare at my tray of food. Ten minutes ago, I was starving. Now, if I eat anything, I'll throw up. It doesn't matter that I got the twins to come to the park on Saturday. None of this would be necessary if I hadn't messed up.

I put my head down on my desk, close my eyes, and go to sleep. I dream about last Friday, and I can't seem to wake myself up. It feels so real until Mrs. Davis shakes me out of that nightmare.

"Come on, Mya. You've been in here long enough. Time to go home. I brought you your books and homework. See you tomorrow."

"Yes, ma'am."

I gather my things and leave in-school detention. I barely get the straps of my backpack on my shoulders when I hear lots of voices outside. There's a crowd of kids, and usually that means there's a fight. I race over to see what's going on. I wiggle through the crowd.

"Excuse me."

When I get to the front, I can't believe my eyes as I listen to Connie going off on Naomi.

"The only reason I'm helping is because it's for the twins! This has nothing to do with you! I wish you weren't even involved!"

Naomi talks back. "Do you think I care about what you wish?"

"I know you don't care about anything or anybody except yourself. You proved that when we were in those pageants together."

Naomi rolls her eyes. "I can't believe you're still mad about that. Get a life, Connie."

"Why don't you get a personality, Naomi?"

The crowd's yelling. *"Fight, fight, fight!"*

I rush in between them. "No! Stop!"

The crowd goes silent. I keep talking. "There's not going to be a fight. Go home. Everybody go home!"

Fish helps me out. "It's over. Get moving!"

Nugget helps, too. "I think I saw Mr. Winky coming this way."

Kids run. In seconds, the area is clear except for Connie, Naomi, Fish, and Nugget and me. I turn to the guys.

"I need to speak with Connie and Naomi alone, okay?"

"Sure, Mya Papaya!"

"See you at home."

Once they're gone, I frown at Connie and Naomi. "What are you doing? What if the twins hear about this? I can't believe it."

Connie rolls her eyes. "Jackson wants to run everything. When I was talking with Lisa, Kenyan, and Johnny, she was supposed to be talking to David, Michael, and Mary Frances about what to bring, and how much help we were going to need. Instead, she decided to call everybody over to where she was standing and leave me out of everything. That's why I don't think I want to be involved in this, Mya. The twins are my friends, and I love them, but I can't work with Jackson."

"I didn't do it on purpose, Connie."

"Right. You think I'm going to believe that?"

I'd give anything to have two hammers, a handful of nails, and that gray gooey stuff Dad gave us in the backyard. I think Connie and Naomi could learn from that lesson. I don't have the stuff. So I tell them the story. I explain what Nugget and I had to do, and what each step meant. Even though Naomi and Connie weren't actually doing the task, I can tell they're listening by the way their expressions change. When I finish, I let them know.

"You may not like each other right now, but one day you may become friends again, and you'll regret this day when you put holes in each other."

We stand in silence. Connie's back is to Naomi,

and Naomi's back is to Connie. I'm standing in the middle, hoping my story makes a difference. I hear a sigh, but I'm not sure who it came from. Suddenly Naomi turns around and talks to Connie's back. There's a whole lot of sadness in her face as she breathes in and out, in and out, before she speaks. And then, she does.

"I'm sorry for the holes I put in you, Connie. Not just the ones from today. All of them."

Naomi takes off toward her home, and she doesn't turn around to look back at us.

Connie's crying, and she runs toward home, too. "I'll talk with you later, Mya."

I don't know if she's happy or still mad. But I do know one thing for sure. Something happened. I think it may have been good.

And I was dead smack in the middle of it.

# Chapter Twenty-Eight

My heart hurts for the twins, Connie, and Naomi, but for the first time in two weeks, I'm excited about going home. As soon as I open the door, I take in a big whiff.

"You smell that, Nugget?"

"Pork chops," he says with a grin.

We both love Mom's pork chops. Maybe she baked a cake, too! I grab my backpack and rush upstairs to get my homework done so it won't be a reason for us to cut our family meeting short.

Two hours later, I hear the front door open, and I know it's Dad. It won't be long now before Nugget and I get a shout to come downstairs. These last two weeks have felt more like two years. I had no idea how important it was for me to feel love and get attention from my family.

And if I hadn't had that talk with Mrs. Davis, I could be heading into a third week of misery. Instead, my heart pumps happiness through my body as I wash my hands for dinner and then go stand near my door and wait.

"Nugget, Mya, come downstairs, please," yells Dad.

I barely beat Nugget into the hallway. I'm sure we sound like a stampede coming down the steps. The delicious aroma of pork chops almost has me floating toward the dinner table. When I get into the dining room, I can't believe my eyes. Mom has cooked a feast, with all my favorites. We're even having tropical punch instead of iced tea! Boo-yang!

Mom brings Macey to the table. She coos at me, and I tell her we'll talk later about my day. I know that's what she wants to hear. After Dad blesses the food, we dig in as if we haven't eaten in a month. Everything tastes so good. Mom and Dad talk about the store and ask Nugget and me about our day. It's small talk. I get it. So I do the best I can to give them the high points, not the low ones. And then

Dad clears his throat.

"Mya, Nugget, Macey, your mom and I have a few things we would like to say to all three of you. Honey, you can go first."

Mom takes my hand and holds it on the table. "Mya, I cried all night. To think that you felt alone and unloved by me—that was the worst thing I could hear. You may not believe this, but you're my best friend. I always wanted a girl, and then I got you. We've done so many things together, but the biggest thing I like is that we cover for each other. Let me give you an example.

"When I was still pregnant with Macey, you needed me to help you with the Wall of Fame game. And then you decided you wanted to enter the chili cook-off, even though I couldn't be there with you. I should have been preparing Macey's room, but I felt you needed me more."

I feel the tears coming, but I try to hold them in and just nod as Mom talks.

"So I chose to help you and do Macey's room later. And then Macey decided to come before I could get her room ready. What did you do? You got your friends together and made Macey's room even more special than I ever could have made it. I was so proud of you, Mya. You stepped in without me asking you to do it."

"Yes, ma'am. I did it because I knew you needed me."

"Yes, I did. But now that Macey's here, she needs me because she can't do anything for herself. Every day I'm trying to do the things I had been doing, keep up with Macey, and try not to be grumpy. Unfortunately, I lost sight of you."

"I forgive you, Mom."

"Thank you, but let me finish. As I thought about the last few weeks, I can see how you would feel that way. I've been so busy. Too busy. When I finally looked at that newspaper you created, I was proud and sad at the same time. Proud that my daughter had created something so special, and sad that I waited so long to take a look at it. Now I know that was your way of trying to get me to see you."

"Yes, ma'am."

"You are magnificent to me, Mya."

I try not to blink because that's going to bring the tears. As Mom talks to me, I realize she's always loved me, and she thinks I am special. It's that she is busy with Macey, who needs her more right now. I love Macey so much, and I want her to get everything she needs while she's a baby, including more of Mom. I totally understand what Mom is saying.

I squeeze Mom's hand. "I'm so glad we can talk together like this, Mom."

She gets up and hugs me. I close my eyes and enjoy every second. When Mom lets go, she wipes a tear from her eye as she looks over at Nugget, and then she takes a seat.

"Son, I know you keep a lot of things in, and you may not tell me everything that I need to know. But if you ever feel as if I'm not giving you enough attention, or if you believe our relationship has changed in any way, please promise me you will come talk to me."

"I promise, Mom."

She leans toward him. He leans toward her, and she kisses him on the forehead.

"Okay, Darrell, I'm finished. You can now have the floor," she says.

Dad stands, paces for a moment, and then crosses his arms over his chest as he talks to me.

"Your mom and I take full responsibility for this. You definitely caught us off guard, but it was the best gift you could've ever given us. Communication is so important. Even if you feel uncomfortable talking about something, you have to know that your mom and I will always be here for you. We love all three of our children, and the very last thing we want you to feel is unloved and invisible. You hear me?"

"Yes, sir."

"You hear me, Nugget?"

"Yes, sir."

Dad smiles. "Okay. So here is what your mom and I have come up with as a plan so that this never happens again. Nugget, the first Saturday of every month belongs to you. That means you get to plan what we will do as a family. Whether it's a movie, going out to the Burger Bar, playing board games, video games, whatever you want to do. We will do that as a family, all day on the first Saturday of every month."

Nugget claps. "Awesome!"

Dad looks my way. "Mya, the second Saturday of every month will belong to you. Everything I told Nugget goes for you. Plan what you want the family to do, and we'll do it. This way, if your mom and I get busy through the week, you know that at least one day a month is devoted to you, and that second Saturday will always be Mya Day."

I clap like Nugget as my feet continue to swing under the table. This is so much better than I could have ever imagined.

Mom adds to what Dad said. "Now this doesn't

mean that your father and I will only listen to you on your day, or do something special with you only on that one day. We're hoping to be more conscious of our time, and devote as much as we can to keeping our family close."

"What about Macey?" I ask.

Mom smiles. "Her day is every day right now. But as she gets older and can do things for herself, she will get the third Saturday in every month. And then, if possible, your dad and I may hire a babysitter so he and I can do something special together on the last Saturday of every month. What do you think?"

"I think that's an awesome idea," I say.

"Me, too," says Nugget. "I've already started thinking of things I want to do."

"Good. Does anyone have anything to add?"

Silence.

"Perfect. I suggest we make this Saturday a family one by attending the Bluebonnet birthday bash at the park! After that, we'll have Nugget's weekend, followed by Mya's. Meeting adjourned!"

I give Mom and Dad big hugs. They deserve it. There's so much love in the room that even Macey coos her approval!

It feels good to get my family back, and if I could, I'd coo, too!

This is the perfect time for me to take a few moments and finish the newspaper. It's not nearly as big as the last two issues, but I think the article is important. We'll give it out on Friday as the last *Texas Taradiddle* newspaper. And I'm hoping I have a few copies to hand out on Saturday at the park, because this party is about us, Bluebonnet. And that makes us special.

# Chapter Twenty-Nine

For the rest of the week, every extra moment we have, Connie, Naomi, and I spend it making plans for the twins' party. Connie doesn't speak directly to Naomi, and Naomi doesn't speak directly to Connie, but we seem to get things done.

Lisa helps us by keeping the twins busy at recess so we can talk to our classmates and make sure they understand what they're supposed to do. We meet with Mrs. Davis. She promises she's going to be at the park on Saturday. Naomi allows us to use her cell to FaceTime with her dad at the car dealership. The three of us ask to borrow tables to hold all of the party goods. He gives them to us, and even throws in red, white, and blue party streamers.

By early Friday morning, I'm exhausted as I stand in front of the school and hand out the last edition of the *Texas Taradiddle* to every kid and adult that walks by. There's no advertising in it. No jokes, no taradiddles. This last edition means something more.

The sun's rays beam down like spotlights on me. Birds chirp springtime music, and it's the perfect mix. I love spring, and I love Bluebonnet.

When I wrote the article for my newspaper, I felt like the loneliest girl in town. And worse, there was nothing special about me. But now, I feel like my bubble guts have turned into smooth waters! I know my parents think I'm special, and I just want everyone to feel like I do!

As I pass out the newspaper before the twins arrive, some people take a copy, while others actually stop and read it. Lisa McKinley's mom walks over to me.

"Mya, did you write this?"

"Yes, ma'am. Connie Tate drew the picture."

"I love it! This article goes right with the theme of Bluebonnet's birthday! I hope everybody thinks about the question you posed. It's a very important one."

"Me, too, Mrs. McKinley."

She smiles. "And thanks for letting Lisa participate. You know, you're one of her favorite friends."

I smile but don't say anything. The more I think about my classmates, and my neighbors, and my family, we're all close, and we're all favorites! Maybe that's what makes our town so awesome.

# THE TEXAS TARADIDDLE

**Mya Tibbs**—Reporter
**Connie Tate**—Photographer & Illustrator

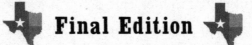

## Final Edition

## Why Is Bluebonnet the Best Town in Texas?

**Homer "Fish" Leatherwood**—You can make good friends in Bluebonnet.

**Mrs. Rodriguez**—There are all kinds of people who live here and we all get along like family.

**Mr. Winky**—There's hope in Bluebonnet. I think there always has been. I hope there always will be.

**Connie Tate**—Bluebonnet is a good town because there is so much beauty here, it is easy to paint without including bluebonnets.

**Mrs. Davis**—Bluebonnet is a good town because the people make it that way. I love living here.

**Darrell Tibbs**—Bluebonnet is where my ancestors began, and where I will continue their hard work.

**Naomi Jackson**—Bluebonnet is the best town because you can be whatever you want to be and it's okay.

**Mya Tibbs**—Bluebonnet is the best town because it's a middle child, in between Dallas and Fort Worth. And it still figured out a way to be special, like me.

Add Your Name_____

Bluebonnet is the best town because _____

_____

# Why Should We Celebrate Birthdays?

Married people celebrate their anniversaries. We celebrate love with Valentine's Day. We even celebrate the day the United States became independent! But none of these celebrations could happen if we as individuals were not here. That is why it is important that we celebrate ourselves as much as we celebrate other things. Two of my favorite friends are celebrating their birthday in April. Skye and Starr Falling will be ten years old. They deserve to be celebrated because they are amazing, and special, and awesome friends. Even though they are twins, I see them separately. And, if you get to know them, you'll see the differences in them, too! So on behalf of the entire planet, I want to wish them the happiest of all birthdays. From Mya

# MYA'S ADVICE COLUMN

In the past few weeks, I've learned how important it is to communicate. Communicating
isn't just talking. It can be expressions on your
face, body movement, a phone conversation, a
letter, hand signals, anything that sends a message to someone else. It is the best way to tell
someone you care about them, or apologize.
So my advice to you is never stop communicating with your family and friends. They deserve
to hear from you when everything is right, but
especially when something is wrong.

I set up a meeting in the Cave after school. We
all pretended like we were leaving, but as soon as
the twins are gone, we all come back in. Mrs. Davis
comes in, too, so she can hear what's going on. Connie, Naomi, and I stand in the middle, while all of
our classmates are seated on benches. I talk first.

"Remember, you should bring three times as
much of your business product to the park tomorrow
as you had in the gym. Is everyone clear on that?"

Heads nod. I keep talking.

"Mary Frances, how's that big birthday card coming?"

"It's ready, Mya. I should be able to get at least five hundred signatures on it from people at the park who want to sign it."

"Okay. We don't have a cake, but Lisa is decorating her awesome cupcakes to look as close to the cake as she can. Thank you, Lisa."

"Anything for the twins," she says.

Everybody claps again.

Naomi puts up her hand. "Everyone needs to be at the park no later than nine thirty tomorrow morning so we can set up. My dad is letting us use three long tables for the party food and presents. Michael, Johnny, David, Kenyan, we need you guys to be there to help him."

"No worries—we'll be there," says Kenyan.

Naomi turns to Connie. "Do you have anything to say?"

Eyes widen. Mouths open. It's no secret that Connie and Naomi are not friends. For Naomi to talk to Connie in that nice tone means the twins' party must be very important to them.

Connie doesn't look at Naomi. "Yes. This is so awesome. We came together for a really good reason, and I'm very happy to be a part of it."

"Me, too," says Mrs. Davis. "Naomi, I will be there to grade you on your presentation. And tomorrow, if I see some of you doing better than you did in the gym last Friday, I will change your grade."

"YAY!!!"

As we leave the school, Naomi waves goodbye, and I wave back to her. Connie and I walk together in silence. We don't have to talk because I know what she's thinking, and she knows what's on my mind. Right before she turns to the left to head home, she hugs me.

"Mya, I'm ready to paint my picture for Bluebonnet."

# Chapter Thirty

On Saturday, I'm up before the sun rises. My family is still asleep, but I've got to be on the move. I cram copies of the last *Texas Taradiddle* into my backpack, along with my red bathroom carpet, before heading to the park. Connie and Naomi greet me with a doughnut and hot chocolate from the Cake Bake. We take our places at the park's entrance and wait on the twins. Suddenly I get a great idea.

"Let's sing a song for the twins! I can make one up to the tune of 'She'll Be Comin' Round the

Mountain When She Comes.' It'll be easy."

"Okay, figure it out and teach it to me," says Connie.

Naomi smiles. "I'm down. Teach it to me, too, Mya."

I sit down on the curb and think about what words would fit in this song to make it about the twins. All kinds of ideas come to me, and I write them all down until the best words are the ones I haven't scratched out. I stand up and teach the song to Connie and Naomi. They catch on fast! I'll wait for the perfect time, and then we'll sing it together to the twins.

The rest of our classmates are already here, too. The tables are up, and Lisa's got cupcakes with black-and-white icing covering one whole table. Susan has her chips and dips, Kenyan brought his fantastic cookies, Johnny brought five jugs of his Jungle Juice! Mary Frances is giving everyone an opportunity to sign the biggest birthday card I've ever seen! David's got the music blaring, and he's already found someone who wants to learn how to dance!

Naomi holds a big bag in one hand. I give away copies of the newspaper. Connie stands next to the most amazing picture I think she's ever drawn.

It's a picture of our town framed with bluebonnets. There's the Cake Bake, and Marco's Grocery, our school, and Tibbs's Farm and Ranch Store. There's the twins' house, and the Burger Bar. And in every open space, there's all kinds of people in all shapes and sizes.

But there's a spot in the picture that I haven't asked Connie about. It has girls playing together. There's a set of twins, and a girl with a bunch of Kleenex, a girl with very blue eyes, a girl with pink cowgirl boots, and two girls with tiaras. I know one of the girls is Naomi.

Is the other one Connie? I know she used to be in pageants.

It's the perfect picture of Bluebonnet, and it's already got a gold star slapped on it! I saw the mayor when he came over and put it there.

As people come in, I give them copies of my very last *Texas Taradiddle*. Even though it's my last one, I believe it is my best one. Connie and I already got an A for our new business from Mrs. Davis. It's no longer about a school project.

This newspaper is about my family and friends.

Down the street, I see Dad pushing Macey in a stroller. Mom's walking beside him, and Nugget's leading the way. When they reach me, I want to hug all of them. So I do. The only one who's upset is Nugget.

"Don't hug me in public, Mya. I've told you about that."

"Sorry," I say with a giggle.

Connie giggles, too.

I pull the stroller top back to take a good look at my little sister. She's all dressed up like a Bluebonnet flower, and as beautiful as she can be.

"You did an awesome job on her costume, Mom," I say.

"Thanks, Mya. She does look cute as a button, doesn't she?"

"Yes, she does," says Connie with a smile.

Dad puts his arm around my shoulders. "I know you're busy, so we're going to take Macey over to the church's tent where they have the Bluebonnet baby garden, and then hang out until your party is over. Then you can come join us. See you later, princess."

I can't help but grin. Dad's given me a new name. Princess.

Connie nudges me. "Here come the guests of honor."

Starr and Skye stroll down the sidewalk in

matching blue dresses. I reach inside my backpack and grab the red bathroom carpet and place it on the ground in front of them.

"You're here!" I say. "Welcome to your party!"

Smiles spread across their faces like sunshine on the first day of spring.

Before they can answer, Naomi opens the bag she was holding and takes out two tiaras and two sashes that say BIRTHDAY GIRL on them. She puts the tiaras on the twins' heads and makes sure they're wearing the sashes perfectly before stepping inside the park. They walk across the red carpet like two queens.

Everybody claps as the twins make their way around the table, hand in hand, and take in everything that was made for them by our classmates. Johnny pours each of us a cup of his Jungle Juice and then makes a toast. "Happy birthday, Skye and Starr!"

We all lift our cups high in the air and chug it down until it's all gone.

"This is the best party I've ever been to in my life," says Skye.

"In my whole life," says Starr.

Enormous applause, bigger than I would have ever expected, comes from behind me. I turn to see crowds of people standing around while more are coming into the park. A van pulls up, and five clowns get out. No way! They ride funny bicycles, make animal balloons, and honk horns at everybody. Soon the music starts, and I'm thinking this place is now a big, big Bluebonnet party!

Looking around the park, there are thousands of people here, eating, dancing, and having fun celebrating Bluebonnet's birthday. But we're taking up an area near the trees and celebrating the twins' birthday in a much smaller way.

Mary Frances holds up a jump rope. Connie grabs one end. Naomi grabs the other. Neither one of them turn the rope, because they're too busy staring at each other. The moment is beyond awkward, and I don't know what to say. I can tell others are feeling the tension between Naomi and Connie, but no one wants to get involved. Not even me.

Connie's face has a whole lot of hurt in it. So does Naomi's. The jump rope isn't moving. Finally Connie breaks the ice.

"I'm the first to go when someone misses," she says.

"Okay," says Naomi with a smile.

I stomp my foot. "So are we jumping rope or what?"

Both Connie and Naomi turn the rope and start singing, "Teddy bear, teddy bear, turn around. Teddy bear, teddy bear, touch the ground." Skye jumps in first, and Starr jumps in with her. Once they jump out, I jump in and jump to the rhythm of the song before jumping out. Mary Frances is next. Even the guys jump rope with us! It's funny at first, but they turn out to be really good at it. David dances as he jumps rope, and we have to make him stop because he's trying to show off. He laughs and gives the guys high fives and fist bumps. I glance over at Connie's picture and realize we're doing exactly what she painted.

Next, we have three-legged races, and the twins win. When it's time to play Toss the Water Balloon, David and Johnny think they're going to win. But when their balloon bursts first, everybody laughs! We laugh even harder when David, Johnny, and Kenyan lose a tug-of-war competition to me, Connie, and Naomi.

Once the twins say they're tired from playing games, we settle down and sing "Happy Birthday" to them as Mrs. Davis lights candles on ten of the cupcakes. The twins blow out the candles, and we clap. Even though their tiaras are crooked, and the sashes have splotches of Johnny's Jungle Juice on them, Skye and Starr look so happy.

The twins are first in line as we each get a paper plate and fill it with tiny hot dogs, chips, dips, cookies, and cupcakes. We sit in the grass and eat, and it's a picnic!

Johnny opens up another jug of his Jungle Juice and pours everybody another cup. That's when I stop him before he makes another toast.

"Hey, everybody, Connie, Naomi, and I would like to sing a song to the twins. Skye and Starr, would you please come over here and stand in front of us."

They do, and the three of us start singing as we hold up our cups.

*"Happy birthday to Bluebonnet and the twins!*
*It's a special town, and they're our special*
    *friends.*
*We'll love Skye and Starr forever,*
*And our city, there's none better,*
*Happy birthday to Bluebonnet and the twins!"*

Everybody joins in, and we sing that verse two more times before we stop and clap! I spot my family not far away. Mom and Dad smile and wave. I wave back. Again, I find myself in the middle of something, but this is so beautiful that I don't want it to ever stop. I hope all of us stay in Bluebonnet and never move away. I hope we stay friends for the rest of our lives. But most of all I hope we remember this Yippee-ki-yay kind of day when our whole town showed up to celebrate something special.

# Acknowledgments

I first want to thank my Lord and Savior, Jesus Christ, for my talent. I love writing, and will continue to write for children as long as I can. My loving husband, Reggie, and my two handsome sons, Phillip and Joshua, are so supportive. Thank you for continuing to encourage me in my endeavors.

I'd also like to thank my critique partners, Laura Ruthven, Varsha Bajaj, Juliet White, and Tim Kane for their help in keeping me on track. Thank you, Dixie, for all your support, love, and friendship.

Jen Rofé, you are the best agent on the planet. We've been together for ten years, as business partners and friends. I hope our relationship continues forever.

Kristin Rens, I cannot thank you enough for all of the amazing questions, comments, and support you have given to me. You are the picture-perfect editor, and I'm so glad you're mine.

And I want to thank all my Strikewriters who have written the amazing stories on my website, for giving me hope that our libraries will continue to thrive as long as they continue to write.

—Crystal Allen

**Crystal Allen** is the author of *How Lamar's Bad Prank Won a Bubba-Sized Trophy*, *The Laura Line*, *The Magnificent Mya Tibbs: Spirit Week Showdown*, and the Sid Fleischman Humor Award–winning *The Magnificent Mya Tibbs: The Wall of Fame Game*. She currently lives in Sugar Land, Texas, with her husband, Reggie, and two sons, Phillip and Joshua. You can visit her website at www.crystalallenbooks .com.

# Don't miss these books by
# CRYSTAL ALLEN!

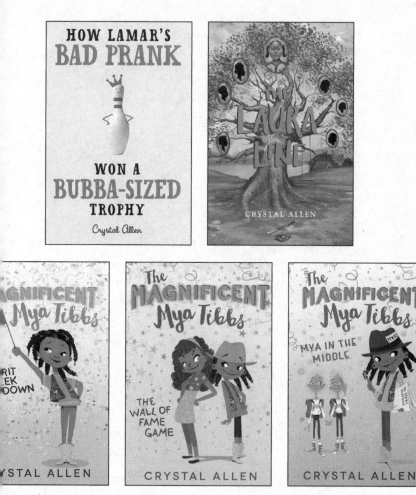